A PREGNANT WIDOW'S AMISH VACATION

EXPECTANT AMISH WIDOWS BOOK 7

SAMANTHA PRICE

AMISH ROMANCE

Copyright © 2016 by Samantha Price

All rights reserved.

No part of this book may be reproduced in any form or by any electronic or mechanical means, including information storage and retrieval systems, without written permission from the author, except for the use of brief quotations in a book review.

Scripture quotations from The Authorized (King James) Version. Rights in the Authorized Version in the United Kingdom are vested in the Crown. Reproduced by permission of the Crown's patentee, Cambridge University Press.

This is a work of fiction. Any names or characters, businesses or places, events or incidents, are fictitious. Any resemblance to actual persons, living or dead, or actual events is purely coincidental.

CHAPTER 1

Know therefore that the Lord thy God, he is God, the faithful God, which keepeth covenant and mercy with them that love him and keep his commandments to a thousand generations;
Deuteronomy 7:9

"I'M NOT GOING out for drinks tonight!" Jane glared at her boss as she sat in safety behind her desk. "It's only been a few months since the accident; it's a miracle I'm still able to function."

Tyrone clenched his square jaw, closed Jane's office door, and then leaned against it, staring at her.

Jane added, "I can't spread myself so thin; there's no time for socializing. Aren't you pleased that I just won the O'Connor account?"

His lips curled, and his arms flung out in the air.

"That's what I've employed you to do, Jane. You were on the trail of that account before... before the accident."

Jane knew Tyrone had been about to say 'before Sean was killed.' "Work's the only thing that's been keeping me going. It's best I don't dwell on... anything else."

"You need to see someone who's qualified in helping people who've been through upheavals."

"I don't need to be psychoanalyzed."

"I'm just looking out for you, and..." Tyrone nodded toward her stomach.

Instinctively, Jane placed her hand on her belly, and said, "We're fine. And I can keep up with all the work. I'll make up for the time I took off."

"You only took one day off and another day for the funeral. That's just not normal."

The advertising business was fierce. There was always someone hungrier coming up behind her, hunting for a promotion, and that's why Jane never felt her position with the company was one hundred percent secure. Besides that, she was an executive when most women who worked at McCloskey and Sullivan were secretaries or assistants. Jane had always found that men were very good at schmoozing and socializing their way up the corporate ladder—it was like a men's club. She knew there was one particular man who had been after her job since he joined the company a year ago—Derek Reynolds.

Tyrone took a step closer. "I think we've become close friends, haven't we?"

Jane looked up at him and had to agree. Tyrone was warm and friendly when he had to be, but he hadn't gotten to where he was by being nice all the time. "Yes, I'd say we're friends."

"As your boss and good friend, I need you to take my advice. I've only got your best interests at heart."

"You want me to take time off? Is that it? I suppose I could, later in the year. Of course, I'll have to take time off when the baby comes—maybe a day or two. I've found a good nanny." Jane bit the inside of her lip as she always did when she lied. She hadn't yet found a nanny, much less thought about finding one. When the time came, she'd call an agency and find one that way.

"You need to come out with me tonight, and the girls. We've all got a surprise arranged for you." He leaned in close enough for her to smell his musky aftershave. "But don't let on that I said anything about a surprise. I wouldn't have told you if you weren't so stubborn. I thought you'd love to have a night out—see the bright lights, listen to some jazz, and enjoy good conversation over a glass of vino."

She leaned back. "I can't drink!"

"Well, scrap that last part. It'll do you good to get out. Before you married Sean you were a party animal."

"I was not! I just went out more before I was married, but I was never one to enjoy going out that much."

"Being married never stopped Sean from doing anything," Tyrone said under his breath.

Jane pouted as she stared into Tyrone's dark brown eyes. She'd ignore what he just said. Even when Sean was alive, Tyrone had always spoken poorly of him—even to his face. At least she knew that Tyrone had been good to her over the past weeks. "Okay. It won't be a late night, will it?" She'd agree to what he wanted, but only because she didn't want to let him down. Then, of course, there was the fact that he *was* her boss.

"When I said it was 'just drinks,' I might have lied." His tanned face broke into a grin.

Jane leaned back in her chair. "What is it—dinner, dancing?"

"Don't worry about it. When I say, 'the girls,' I'm including Derek."

"Derek?" That was the best reason she'd heard *not* to go.

"Don't be like that. I don't know why you two can't get along. I've got great things planned for him."

Jane blew out a deep breath. If she didn't go, Derek would go out with them and then he'd get even friendlier with the girls in the office. Also, he'd try to weasel his way further into Tyrone's good books.

"I think his work is substandard." This time, she bit her lip and frowned when she heard herself lie. Derek's work was quite good—annoyingly so.

"Forget him and anyone else. Tonight is about you."

"What's it all about? What have you got arranged?

In my condition, I can't have a shock." She patted her stomach thinking of the upheavals she'd had just a few months before. Sean had come home and announced he was leaving her; he'd been having an affair for a year and was running away with the woman, whom Sean had told her was named Ralene. Just hours after he'd left, the police knocked on her door to inform her that her husband and the female passenger in his car had both been killed in an automobile accident.

"You'll see. Trust me. I'll take you there and deliver you safely home when it's over."

Jane pressed her lips firmly together. She knew Tyrone had always had a soft spot for her, but then again, she knew he wouldn't do anything about it in her current vulnerable state. She nodded. "Okay." She'd miss out on her normal nightly routine— a hot bath, and then watching something mindless on TV until she fell asleep.

Tyrone flashed a dazzling smile. He knew he was a handsome man, and used his looks to full advantage in his business life as well as his personal life. "Excellent! Get ready to have some fun."

Jane sighed. "I'll be raising a child on my own soon. I've got too much on my plate to think about fun." She looked down at her stomach. "I can't have fun."

"You said 'yes,' so you can't back out now."

"All I want to do is go home and get into a hot bath." She stared into Tyrone's face hoping he'd relent.

When he said nothing, she continued, "What about we leave it for next week?"

"No! Definitely not! Everyone's worried about you. I'm taking charge tonight."

"I think I'm doing okay. It's nice of people to be concerned—but I'll get through it in time."

"It's all arranged; I told everyone you'd be there. Everyone's put a lot of effort into being there."

Jane sighed. If she said any more, she'd sound ungrateful. "What time?"

"Right after work. I'll come and get you at five."

"It won't be a late night will it?"

He smiled, and his bright brown eyes crinkled at the corners. "Trust me."

When he walked out of her office, she touched the space bar of her computer to bring it back to life. What if she'd married Tyrone instead of Sean? She could've had either man back then, but she'd chosen Sean because she'd thought he was the more reliable one of the two. It turned out that she couldn't have been more wrong.

She'd heard rumors of Sean's affairs shortly after they married, but she never found evidence of that being true. Stooping to the lowest of the low, she'd even checked his phone and the emails on his computer hoping to find the truth, but they had revealed nothing.

It was only when Sean told her that he was leaving her did the truth come out. He'd been carrying on an affair with Ralene. For a whole year! Now, Jane's child had been conceived while he'd been involved with another woman. Jane would never forgive Sean for that. When he'd walked out after his confession about the affair, she'd been too numb to cry. Jane only cried when the police sat her down and told her about the accident. The chilling truth was that she might have been able to stop him from leaving her. He'd always wanted a child and she'd always refused. She'd found out she was pregnant two months before he left, and she wasn't sure why she had kept it secret. If she'd told him about the baby, maybe he wouldn't have left her for Ralene and he'd be alive today.

Jane's child would be fatherless. There would be no hope of Sean ever coming home begging for forgiveness. Neither would there be any chance of their child getting to know him. Sean was there one minute and gone the next. It was hard to come to terms with what had happened—it didn't feel like it was real.

Jane had no doubt that Tyrone would wait a suitable time, and then he'd make his move and ask her on a date. That is, unless someone else caught his eye in the meantime. One thing was for certain, Jane did not want another man who would cheat on her—and she knew she couldn't be certain of that with Tyrone. The thing that saddened Jane the most was that her child would be raised in a single-parent family just as she'd been. Jane wanted something better for her child than experiencing the pain she still felt, craving a father—to ask question after question about the man she'd never met.

Hoping that one day he'd come to the door, and say, *'I am your father.'*

After she had wiped away tears with the back of her hand, she pressed the computer's space bar once more. She glanced at the time on the top right of her computer screen. *One hour to go before five.* She had to get on with the O'Connor account. The more work she did on it today, the less she would have to do tomorrow. With Derek ready to pick up any of the slack she left, she couldn't afford to leave any room for him to weasel his way in.

CHAPTER 2

As the cold of snow in the time of harvest,
so is a faithful messenger to them that send him:
for he refresheth the soul of his masters.
Proverbs 25:13

ONCE THEY WERE in the taxi, Jane said to Tyrone, "I thought you said five. It's already five thirty." Jane was a little annoyed. He'd told her it wouldn't be a late night and now she was going to get home half an hour later since they were already behind time.

He shook his head staring at the phone in his hands. "Sorry. I've just texted everyone and they're all there waiting."

"They should be, because we're late." She folded her arms across her chest and stared out the window. "I hope this isn't a thing where someone jumps out of a cake, or I get a stripper gram or something like that."

"The girls just want to do something nice for you. Has anyone ever done anything nice for you?"

She stared at him wondering how to answer him. When he stared back at his phone, she pushed her dark hair behind her ears.

Pulling his eyes from his phone, Tyrone smiled at her and grabbed her hand.

She cleared her throat and then pulled her hand back. "Are we going far?"

"Just around the corner," he said. "We could've walked there, but I thought in your condition you would've preferred to go by cab."

"That's right. I've never liked walking, even when I wasn't in this condition," she joked.

"Here we are." He paid the cab driver and then raced around to open the car door for her.

She stepped out to see a wine bar/restaurant where she'd been with the girls once before. "I like this place."

"That's why we're here," he said guiding her out of the car.

They walked in and joined the girls who had a booth to one side of the room. Then she spotted short, balding Derek, sitting on the outermost seat and grinning like a fool. Derek jumped up and greeted her with a kiss on the cheek, and the girls followed his lead.

When they were seated, Tyrone asked everyone, "Have we got drinks ordered?"

"Yeah, we've got drinks coming," one of the girls said.

"Good." Tyrone turned to Jane who had just sat down. "What would you like?"

"Lime and soda for me thanks."

Once they each had a drink in their hands, Tyrone said, "Now for the big surprise. I won't waste any time since I'm already in trouble for being late. Here's to Jane!" He pulled a white envelope out of his pocket and handed it to her.

"What's this?" she asked, turning it over and looking for some clue to what it was.

Derek, her nemesis, was the only one who answered. "Everyone's chipped in and we're sending you on a vacation." He sat there looking pleased with himself.

By the smile on Derek's face, she knew exactly what was going on. He'd set her up. Time away from work was the worst thing right now. What would happen to the O'Connor account?

Once Jane looked at all the smiling faces staring at her and waiting for a reaction, she smiled. Maybe she *could* do with a little time away from everything. She hoped the vacation might be a Mediterranean cruise, or maybe a cabin on a beach island.

"Open it and see," Tyrone said.

"I will. Thank you, everyone! This is such a lovely

surprise." She'd pretend to go along with it and then she'd find some way to get out of it. Unless of course, it was a Mediterranean cruise, or a cruise around the Greek Islands. She opened the envelope and pulled out a card. She read that it was a stay at a bed and breakfast in Lancaster County. It seemed like Derek wanted her far, far away. "A B&B! Lovely!" She put on her best false smile and looked around at the girls. "Thank you."

Tyrone said, "Did you see how long it's for?"

Please don't be for more than a week. "Oh no, I didn't." Jane looked down at the card again, and calculated the dates to see that it was a whole four weeks long. "Four weeks?" She looked across at Tyrone and knew her face said it all.

"You need it!" He swallowed a mouthful of his drink. "What's more, I'm paying you for this vacation and I'm not including it in your vacation bank. You'll still be entitled to another four weeks vacation as per your employment package."

"Thank you." She smiled because she knew Tyrone thought he was doing something nice.

"You'll enjoy the peace and quiet and come back relaxed and fresh," Jenny, her personal assistant, said.

Jane nodded. "It's truly wonderful of everyone. Thank you."

"The main person you have to thank is Derek; it was his idea. And he's offered to look after the O'Connor account while you're gone."

"The O'Connor account is mine," she blurted out without thinking.

"Relax!" Tyrone said. "No one is taking it from you; he's only helping."

Derek smiled and his double chin wobbled as he said, "I'm not taking anything away from you, Jane." He reached over for some fries that were in a bowl in the middle of the table.

As the girls chattered away, Jane looked into her glass wishing there was something stronger in it than soda. This was a deliberate plot; a deliberate plot against her. She wondered how long Derek had been scheming. Jane gave him a sideways glance before she pleaded with Tyrone. "I can take this later in the year, can't I? After we have the O'Connor account up and running properly?"

"No! You have to take it now—the dates are on here." Tyrone tapped the card, which was now on the table in front of her.

She picked it up to see how soon she'd have to go. *Is Tyrone crazy?* "That's the day after tomorrow. I can't possibly get organized in that time."

"Yes, you can."

"I'll help you," Jenny said.

She wondered what other excuse she could make. No matter how bad things had gotten for her in her life, she'd always had a good job ever since she'd finished college, which she'd worked her way through. Now, however, her seemingly secure position with the company seemed uncertain, with Derek in the wings ready to pounce. He'd already managed to contrive a plot to get her out of the way, and if she was gone for four weeks, she might not have a job to come back to. Tyrone wouldn't hesitate to give Derek her position if he thought that was best for the company.

"Thank you everyone; this is very lovely and a very kind gesture." When she realized that was the second time she'd thanked them in five minutes, she hoped she didn't sound too false. "I might sound ungrateful, or a little strange, it's just the suddenness of it all. I'm overwhelmed." She looked down at the card again and then picked it up. "Has anyone been to this place?"

"Derek's been there and he says it's wonderful," Karen, one of the secretaries, said.

"You've been there?" Jane asked Derek.

"I have; it's a very special place. You'll see what I mean when you get there. You'll be ringing me up thanking me." Derek leaned forward and seeming almost genuine, said, "You'll be able to relax, regroup, and recuperate. There are things to do or you can choose to do nothing."

Jane nodded, knowing it was already too late; nothing she could do or say would make a difference. "That was nice of you, Derek." He seemed sincere; maybe she'd misjudged him. Time away from everything might do her good. Home was never the same since Sean's death—amongst all his things, all of them reminders of him. Maybe getting away and finding the 'old Jane' was what she really needed to do. She'd spent so much time trying to juggle her career demands and make Sean happy, that she'd lost 'herself' in the process. *Perhaps in these four weeks, I could try to become the person I once was, before I married Sean.*

CHAPTER 3

*For unto you it is given in the behalf of Christ,
not only to believe on him,
but also to suffer for his sake.*
Philippians 1:29

IT WAS a long bus ride from New York to Lancaster County. Why couldn't they have sent her somewhere she could have flown? Or perhaps there were flights between New York and somewhere close to Lancaster County—she didn't know, hadn't thought to check during the rush to get ready. Lancaster County was never a vacation destination that she would've chosen.

Once she arrived, she stepped off the bus, collected her suitcase and headed to the taxi rank to wait in the short queue. When she got into a taxi, she handed the driver the address.

As the taxi ventured further into the countryside, she had to admit that she felt better. Perhaps it was leaving all her problems behind her, but then again, sooner or later, she'd have to face reality again.

"There you go, Ma'am," the taxi driver said as he drove up a long driveway.

Jane had been lost in her own world. "Is this it?" she asked looking at a large house, which was undergoing some building work, going by the scaffolding up one side.

"This is one of the best Amish bed and breakfasts around here."

"Amish?" Her stomach lurched and she hoped she wouldn't be sick. "Stop the car!"

He slammed on the brakes fifty yards from the house. He turned around and looked at her. "This is the address you gave me."

"No... no one told me it was Amish."

"You're slap bang in the middle of Amish country here."

Jane put a hand over her stomach, as she grew angry. "Derek!" she said in a controlled voice despite wanting to scream. There was no doubt in her mind anymore that Derek had done this deliberately after having learned of her issue with the Amish.

"Do you want to go somewhere else, Ma'am? I could take you to a hotel back in town."

"Um…" She was too tired to travel all the way back. And if she went home, that would make her boss unhappy, which would immediately give Derek the upper hand. The whole thing was a cruel slap in the face.

She certainly couldn't tell Tyrone that Derek had done this deliberately. Besides sounding unprofessional, she didn't want Tyrone to know that she saw Derek as a threat. And where Derek was concerned, she preferred not to let him know that she was on to him. She'd have to pretend she liked it here and, above all, that she was having a nice time. That was the only way to beat Derek at his own game.

"Well, Miss?" the taxi driver asked.

She snapped back to reality and looked at the driver. "I'll stay!"

"Don't get out here. I'll take you closer to the house." He drove the remaining few yards to the entrance.

She paid the driver, and he took her suitcase right to the door. Once he'd driven away, she took a deep breath and pushed the door open.

"Hello! We've been waiting for you; that is, if your name is Jane Walker."

Jane looked at the friendly woman dressed in full Amish clothing and forced a smile. The woman was wearing a starched white cap, a white apron over a dark blue long dress that ended mid-calf, and on her black stockinged feet were black lace-up boots. She appeared to be in her late fifties to mid-sixties, but perhaps Amish women looked older than they really were, as they didn't have the benefit of using makeup or hair dyes, or wearing fashionable clothes. Her ruddy face was full and free of lines except at the corners of her eyes.

This woman can't be held responsible for what happened, Jane reminded herself. "Yes, I'm Jane."

"I'm Mrs. Yoder, the owner of the B&B."

"Nice to meet you."

"Your luggage is outside?" Mrs. Yoder asked.

"Yes, I've only got the one bag, but it's rather heavy."

The woman yelled loudly, "Tobias."

Jane had jumped at the sudden outburst. Then she waited for someone to appear. It didn't take long for an old man to walk into the room.

He looked at her and nodded. "Hello."

"Hello. I'm Jane."

"This is Tobias Yoder, my husband. He'll get your suitcase. The suitcase is outside Tobias."

"I'm Tobias as you've already heard," he said with a lopsided boyish grin before he walked past her.

"Nice to meet you," Jane said as he headed out the door. If Mrs. Yoder hadn't introduced him as her husband, Jane would've thought he was her father. He had to be many years her senior.

"I suppose you should call me Lizzie if you'd prefer,

rather than calling me Mrs. Yoder. I think the days are over where adults called adults by their last names."

"Okay, Lizzie. Call me Jane."

Tobias came back inside carrying the heavy suitcase effortlessly and then walked right past the two women.

"Just the one suitcase for a four week stay?"

"Yes. It holds a lot. It's quite heavy."

"You'll be staying in the Rose Room. I've given all my rooms names of flowers." Lizzie giggled like a young girl. "I hope Mr. Reynolds told you about the accommodation?"

Reynolds. That was Derek's last name. "He didn't tell me much about it. Is there something I should know?"

"I explained to Mr. Reynolds that we aren't fully open again until we get through with the renovations. He insisted on us having you here, and we did have the Rose Room completed, so I hope that's all right? Didn't he inform you of that?"

"No. He didn't. So I'll be the only guest, is that what you're saying?"

"That's correct, and through the day, there might be construction noise and a bit of dust, but he insisted you wouldn't mind."

"That makes sense." *Yes, it made sense that Derek had sent her to a place she already didn't like, and on top of that she wouldn't be able to rest or relax!* "This four week vacation is my special holiday from work. Everyone was kind enough to put in for it since they thought I needed a rest."

A young girl came running into the room and started talking.

"Mind your manners, Gia. This is Mrs. Walker." Lizzie looked up at Jane. "This is Gia."

The young girl looked around six or seven years of age. She was wearing Amish clothes just like Lizzie's, but no cap.

"Hello, Gia." Jane smiled at the young girl.

Gia smiled back to reveal a missing front tooth. "Hello, Mrs. Walker. Are you staying here?"

Her missing tooth appeared to give Gia a lisp.

"I'm staying here tonight." She wasn't sure if she'd stay there if there were going to be constant hammering and dust. Surely that would be something that Tyrone would understand. She continued to speak to Gia. "Your mother was kind enough to make room for me even though the building is undergoing renovations."

"I'm her grandmother," Lizzie was quick to say.

"I'm sorry," Jane said.

"You have pretty pink lips," Gia said staring up at her.

"Thank you."

"Gia lives with us here." Lizzie went on to tell Jane what time the meals were and then handed her a booklet.

"Thank you. It certainly is a lovely place you have

here."

"Thank you. We like it. It's been in my husband's family for generations. It's got lovely gardens and a river. There are many pleasant walks to take down by the river and around the fields."

"That's wonderful. I'll keep that in mind. And how far is it to town?" Jane knew she would go crazy not seeing another soul for weeks, apart from Amish people—that was, if she did decide to stay. She looked at Mrs. Yoder eagerly awaiting her answer.

"It's only five minutes in a taxi. And we've got the phone connected, so you can call out any time you like. We've got a lovely village and shops."

"Oh, you've got electricity?" It hadn't occurred to Jane that they might not have electricity and phone connected. Jane was pleased about that at least.

"We do. Amish businesses are mostly allowed electricity. It's a necessity of doing business."

"That's good. I'd like to have a look in the town I just drove through. Maybe I'll do that tomorrow."

"We have two different townships. The one you rode through is five minutes away, and the other is about ten minutes in the other direction. We're nicely placed between the two."

Mrs. Yoder was starting to sound like a promotional blurb.

Tobias returned. "I'll take you to your room. Follow me."

Jane walked with Tobias down the hallway toward

the Rose Room. "This is the only room we have that didn't need renovation. We weren't going to let it out until everything was finished, but your friend was insistent."

"Yes, I heard; he can be like that. He's very determined." She opened her purse and handed Tobias money.

He waved his hands. "That's not necessary. Everything's been paid for."

A small voice sounded. "Excuse me." They both turned to see Gia. "*Mammi* said to bring you these. It's cake and a sandwich in case you're hungry. And fresh milk in case you want to make a cup of tea in your room."

Mammi must be Amish for the word Grandmother, Jane thought.

Tobias said, "That's only if you want to have tea in your room. Otherwise, you're welcome to use the kitchen at any time."

"Thank you," she said to Tobias before she looked at Gia. "You're a big girl to carry all that in by yourself." Gia smiled at her and then Jane asked Tobias, "Where's the kitchen?"

"Gia, would you like to show Mrs. Walker the kitchen?"

Gia nodded. "It's this way."

Jane followed the girl down the wide hall until they came to the end. She went through a door that opened up into a wide kitchen with open hearth and huge fireplace.

"It's quite cozy, but in a big way," Jane said.

At that moment, the door at the far end of the kitchen was flung open.

"Dat!" Gia ran to greet a large-framed sweaty Amish man in a wide-brimmed black hat.

"Don't get too close, Gia. My clothes are dusty." He looked up at Jane. "Oh, I'm sorry. I didn't know we had guests."

"I'm Jane."

He nodded. "I'm Zac, generally known around here as 'the son.'"

"He's my *Dat*," Gia said with a beaming smile.

"You haven't been bothering Mrs...." He looked up at Jane.

"It's actually Ms. Walker." She had just decided to go by Ms. at that moment since she didn't have a husband any longer and she didn't feel like a 'Miss.' Miss seemed a term for a younger woman.

"Have you been bothering, Ms. Walker, Gia?"

"Nee, Dat. I don't bother people."

"She's been a good help to me. She's showing me around," Jane said.

"I see. Well, good girl, Gia. *Mammi* is putting you to work."

Gia smiled up at her father, and he patted her on her head in a gentle and caring fashion. The love of a father was something Jane's child would never know—that was something beyond Jane's control. Her child would live out the kind of life she'd had–a fatherless one.

Zac looked across at her while taking off his coat. "I remember now. You must be the mystery guest?"

"Mystery guest? I don't know about that. Well, I suppose I am."

He took off his hat, placed it on a peg by the door and shook out his thick dark hair. Zac was full-faced as his mother was, and although he wasn't a handsome man, he exuded a quiet confidence that made him instantly appealing.

"I was told about you a few days ago. There was supposed to be no one staying here for the next month. I asked them—my parents to keep the calendar clear so I could get in and get some work done."

The way his brown eyes bore through her made her feel as though she were intruding. In her defence, she said, "I didn't book my stay. People from work thought I needed to get away. They booked it and surprised me. It would've been rude to say 'no.'"

"So you didn't want to come here?"

She shook her head. "No. I didn't want to go anywhere. This was forced on me." She stared at him as though to say, *'happy now?'*

"Well, here you are." He shook his head. "I'm going to have to make the best of it." There was no apology in his tone—his words said it all—she was unwelcome.

The son hadn't inherited any manners from his

parents, both of whom had been welcoming and friendly.

To heck with it, she was tired of being pushed around and trying not to upset people. She'd speak her mind. "It seems you don't want me here?"

He screwed his face up and scratched his chin. "As long as you don't complain about me hammering at six in the morning."

"Six? How is it a holiday for me if you start making loud noises that early? I've come here to rest, not to be tortured."

He shook his head again. "I can't believe this is happening. I've only got a narrow timeframe to do so much work. I don't think I'll finish it in time."

"Maybe you should talk to your parents about that."

"They're the problem." He looked down at his daughter. "You go back to *Mammi*."

When Gia left the room, Jane wondered if he might apologize for his rudeness that made her feel so unwelcome.

"I thought I'd finished for the day, but now that you're here, I won't be able to waste the daylight."

Jane frowned. "What do you mean?"

"Don't worry. It's not your problem. I'm just talking to myself." He turned around, grabbing his coat and hat before he pulled open the door.

Jane opened her mouth to say something, but he was gone before she thought of a reply. Zac had closed the door a little too loudly—she was certain of that.

She marched to the window and looked out to see him striding toward the barn. He rammed on his hat and then pushed his arms into his coat. The man had no manners. His one saving grace, in Jane's book, was that he was loving to his daughter.

CHAPTER 4

I will go in the strength of the Lord God:
I will make mention of thy righteousness, even of thine only.
Psalm 71:16

ALONE IN THE KITCHEN, Jane sat down on a stool by the kitchen counter. If Gia lived there in that very house, that meant Zac and his wife did too, and that would mean she'd have to sit at the same table with Zac at dinner. Lizzie had told her that they all ate at the one table.

Jane wondered if Zac was nice to his wife and spoke tenderly as he'd spoken to Gia. If so, she would be jealous and make no excuses for it. All she'd wanted from Sean was to be loved fully and completely, and he'd failed her. Now Sean was dead; she couldn't ask him why he'd treated her so poorly and sought comfort in another woman's arms. Was there something about her that Sean had found awful? She was no supermodel —Jane knew that, but she wasn't ugly either. Jane figured herself moderately attractive.

Knowing the kitchen would soon be abuzz with dinner preparations, Jane headed back to her room. Once she was there, she unpacked her clothes while thinking about vacation destinations she'd rather be at. If only the view from her window was one of golden sand and crashing waves, rather than green rolling acres that went on and on into oblivion.

The last place she would've chosen was anywhere near the Amish, but now she was stuck there. Too tired to do anything about it, she decided she would stay and try to make it work. If she left, Derek would get exactly what he wanted—satisfaction. She would call or email work the very next day and tell them how much she loved the place. That would take the wind out of Derek's sails. Jane chuckled as she closed the last of her underwear into one of the dresser drawers.

She opened the cupboard door and pushed in her empty suitcase. Once she closed the door, she lay down on the bed. This bed was higher than her bed at home, and it was comfortable, neither too hard nor too soft. The room was clean and had everything except for a TV, although that didn't matter because she'd brought books with her that she'd never had time to read at home.

Jane closed her eyes, intent on quieting her mind, but a mental list of things she had to do ran through her head. There was the life insurance company she had to call, and send them details of Sean's death. Jane hoped the payout would be a sizeable sum, she couldn't remember the figure, but she knew it would be more than enough to pay off the mortgage on her apartment. After a few years' work, she might be able to retire with enough to send her child to a good school.

Before long, Jane was asleep. The next thing she knew, someone was knocking on her door talking about dinner.

"I'm coming!" Jane called back. She rolled over on her side and pushed herself to a seated position. Knowing she would have to leave a shower until after dinner, she quickly fixed her hair and makeup. When she had made herself look decent, she walked out of the room in the clothes she'd been wearing all day.

Jane had assumed they'd be eating in the large eat-in kitchen, but when she walked in, she could see she'd been wrong. There were two young Amish women working frantically.

"Where do I go for dinner?" Jane asked one of the women.

"I'll take you to the dining room."

"Yes, of course, the dining room." No one had mentioned anything about a dining room. But then again, she hadn't read the detailed brochure that Lizzie had handed her.

"This way." The woman wiped her hands on a tea towel and walked past Jane. Then the young lady took her back down the hall, through the reception area and up a couple of steps.

"This is a long way from the kitchen, isn't it?"

The young lady giggled. "There's a passageway from the kitchen to the dining room and it connects the two."

"That makes more sense. It's like a horseshoe-shape?"

"Yes." The woman stood back once they came to a well-lit room. Jane walked into the dining room to see the family sitting around a large round table. The white tablecloth, the white and blue china dishes were grander than Jane would've expected from a humble Amish establishment, but then again it wasn't the Amish they were catering to—this was for the tourists.

"There you are," Lizzie said when Jane walked into the room.

"I'm sorry I'm late. I didn't know where the dining room was. I thought you would've eaten in the kitchen."

Young Gia laughed and when her father touched her on the shoulder, she stopped.

"The food smells amazing." As Jane sat down, she saw the food was in white china covered bowls in the centre of the table.

"We have two girls who do the cooking for us now that..." Lizzie looked embarrassed and didn't finish what she was about to say. "This is Sarah and the other girl we have working for us is Mary."

Jane turned around and nodded hello to Sarah and she nodded back. Jane wondered what Lizzie had been about to say? Now that what?

Tobias said, "Yes, even though we've got the place under construction we still have the girls cooking for us because my wife's hands are riddled with arthritis."

Lizzie looked down at her hands. "Yes they are." She spread her hands and showed them to Jane.

Jane gazed at Lizzie's knobbly hands. "Are they painful?" Something was going on—something that the Yoders didn't want to discuss in her presence.

"They are painful sometimes, but only when I move them. It helps if I keep them warm."

"We generally close our eyes and give thanks for the food before we eat," Tobias said.

"Don't let me stop you," Jane said. "I say grace sometimes before I eat. Do we hold hands?"

Zac frowned at her, and said, "No." He shook his head while Gia gave Jane a big smile.

When everyone closed their eyes, Jane followed. She waited for someone to speak, but no one did. After a while, she opened her eyes to see that Lizzie now had hers open, and Tobias was just opening his.

Sarah, who'd been standing back, stepped forward to serve the food onto the plates.

"This is a typical Amish meal. I thought we'd have this tonight." Lizzie said.

"What is it exactly?" Jane asked.

Tobias answered, "We've got pork chops, sauerkraut, and potatoes. If you don't eat pork, we've got fried chicken. We have two varieties of meat at every meal."

"You aren't vegetarian, are you?" Lizzie asked.

"No, I like my meat too much."

"Good. We like to know by ten every morning if you aren't eating dinner with us. We have a form for you to fill in and leave at the kitchen if you're dining with us. All meals are included, but often our guests make other arrangements."

"Okay." Jane nodded. "The food looks lovely and so fresh." The carrots were almost red and the peas and beans were dark green.

As Lizzie went on to explain about the mashed potatoes and how the meal was cooked, and how they'd grown all their vegetables in their garden, Jane was feeling too miserable to listen. Every now and again, she'd smile and nod in the appropriate places wondering why Lizzie was still talking. Surely the food would get cold.

When everyone at the table was silent, Jane knew that was her time to make a comment. "Ah, well, it looks and smells delicious."

"The proof is in the eating," Zac said. "Help yourself please, Jane."

"Okay."

"I'll give you a hand," Tobias said as he stood and proceeded to heap food onto Jane's plate.

"Not too much. I can't eat a lot at one time."

When everyone had food on their plates, Lizzie looked at Jane. "Go ahead and start eating."

"Okay." Jane smiled at everyone before she took a mouthful of mashed potatoes. She nodded as she ate. Her obvious delight over the potatoes seemed to please everyone, and they began eating as well.

"Will Mr. Walker be joining you?" Zac asked before he spooned a forkful of potato into his mouth.

Lizzie looked at Zac and said quietly, "The booking was only for one."

Jane was taken aback by Zac's question, but she'd been wondering where Gia's mother was, so he was being just as curious. Perhaps Zac's wife was one of the women in the kitchen, but wouldn't she have eaten with the family? She cleared her throat. "Mr. Walker is not in the picture."

Zac raised his eyebrows. "I'm sorry. I didn't mean to be nosey."

Gia looked up at her father. "You're always telling me not to be nosey, *Dat*."

"You're quite right, Gia, and do you remember what else I always tell you?"

"Don't talk at the dinner table?" Gia asked.

"That's right."

"Sorry, *Dat*."

"There you go again, talking at the table."

Gia smiled and pressed her lips together with her fingers.

"That's better, now not another word," Zac said.

Lizzie added, "Dinner is adults' time to speak, Gia."

"Have you had the B&B for a long time?" Jane asked Lizzie before she remembered that she'd already been told that it had been in Tobias' family for many generations.

"It was Tobias' great-grandfather's. He built the original house. At the time, there was a lot more land than it has now. Various parcels of land were given to the children over the years when they married. Now it stands on just over sixty acres."

"That's a lot of land," Jane said.

Tobias said, "This used to be a farm-stay B&B a few years back."

That would make perfect sense. Derek would've found out she didn't like being around farms and getting dirty. "You mean the people who stayed here would have to do farm work?"

Zac laughed loudly. "I can see by the look on your face that you can't think of anything worse."

"No," Tobias said. "They could do work if they wanted to have the real farm experience, but we've never forced anyone to help out." Tobias chuckled.

"Don't mind them, Jane. How would you know if you've never been here before?"

Jane smiled at Lizzie. "I've never stayed at one of

these places—a B&B, I mean. I've always stayed at hotels."

"Five stars I'd guess," Zac said. When Jane looked at him, he said, "That's a compliment, because you look like the kind of lady who would have the very best of everything."

"Stop it, Zac! I don't know what's gotten into you," Lizzie said.

"Leave him alone, Lizzie. Miss Walker knows he's only having a laugh." Tobias' blue-green eyes twinkled.

"Yes, that's quite all right. I know a joke when I hear one." *And Derek sending me here is a joke—a joke on me for coming here and leaving him at work with the O'Connor account.*

"I'm sorry, Ms. Walker will you forgive me?" He placed his hand over his heart, but she was certain from the look in his eyes that he didn't mean a word of his apology.

"Of course. There's nothing to forgive. Nothing at all." She wouldn't let Zac see that she was bothered by all his nonsense. Jane turned to face Lizzie. "This food is delicious. It's the nicest meal I've had for some time.

"What brings you here by yourself Ms. Walker?" Zac asked.

His father gave him a sideways glance as though Zac had been instructed not to ask the guests their personal details.

"Please, Zac, Tobias, you can call me Jane. It's rather an enforced vacation, as I told you earlier today. I work hard at my job and my boss made me take a break for the next few weeks." She looked down at her food annoyed with herself for agreeing to a four-week vacation. How did Derek pull it off and do so without someone in the office whispering about it and telling her what he was up to? Unless the girls in the office were now on *his* side.

"You look sad for someone having a vacation," Zac commented. "Aren't vacations supposed to be happy?"

"Zac," his father said in a low voice as if to say, 'mind your own business.'

"It's the first vacation I've had since my husband died; I suppose that's why I don't look happy. It's been quite an adjustment."

Zac looked surprised.

"My *mudder* died," Gia said.

That explained the absence of Zac's wife, the little girl's mother. "Oh, I'm so sorry to hear that. We have something in common, Gia. We've both lost people dear to us."

Gia's eyes widened. "Maddie says *Mamm* didn't go to heaven."

Lizzie gasped. "Gia! Don't talk like that."

"Who's Maddie?" Zac asked his daughter.

The dinner conversation was suddenly getting more interesting and Jane was glad the focus was on someone else. Lizzie and Tobias were definitely uncomfortable with the direction the conversation was taking.

"Maddie is the Willems' *dochder*," Lizzie said. "And I'll be having a word with Maddie's *mudder*."

"Is your husband in heaven, Ms. Walker?" Gia asked.

"We don't ask people things like that," Zac said.

Gia sighed and looked at the food on her plate. "I was just asking," she said in a tiny voice.

"Eat your food," Zac said sternly. "No talking at the table. You'll do well to remember that."

A change in the conversation was needed, and then the next question was directed at Jane.

"What kind of work do you do that keeps you working so hard?" Zac asked.

"I'm in advertising." Looking at their blank faces, she added, "I'm an advertising executive. I pitch campaigns to firms looking to sell more of their products—companies such as airlines or department stores." Jane hated the out-dated word, 'pitch,' but thought that might be a term that the Amish had heard before.

Lizzie nodded as though she understood and Tobias continued eating without saying a word.

"Sounds impressive. We should be pleased to have you in our little corner of the world." Zac smiled at her.

"And we are pleased," Lizzie said staring at Jane.

Tobias cleared his throat. "You might be able to help us with our new campaign and our relaunch party."

Lizzie looked open-mouthed at her husband. "You can't ask that of Miss Walker. She's our guest."

Jane wanted to correct Lizzie and tell her that Miss was a sexist term and she preferred to go by, 'Ms,' but because she didn't want to risk offending, she let it go. "I'd be happy to. I prefer to do something all the time—I like to keep occupied. And please, call me Jane."

"We'd pay you of course," Tobias said.

Jane shook her head. "No need to do that. You'd be doing me a favor—honestly."

Tobias chuckled and Jane noticed that Lizzie shot him a look of disdain before she turned back to Jane. "We'll pay you," she said with a final nod.

"No!" Jane shook her head. She'd be pleased for the distraction that might save her from going stir crazy.

"We'll see. We'll come to some arrangement. I guess we shouldn't talk about such things at the table."

"This food is wonderful." Jane said knowing that the Amish food was an attraction for tourists visiting the region. It was all over the brochures she'd skimmed through in her room. "And the rooms—well, my room is clean, bright and spotless. I was really impressed when I walked in."

"Was your husband also in advertising?" Tobias asked.

"You don't have to answer that." Lizzie shot her husband another glare.

"That's okay. I don't mind talking about him. It might do me good." She shook her head. "He was in sales. He worked for a car company, and he traveled a lot." *Yes, and that was a perfect cover for his sordid affair.*

Once they'd finished their main meals, the two women who'd been in the kitchen came out of nowhere to clear the dishes. Once the dishes were gone, the dessert was served.

"My goodness! I hadn't quite expected to have so much food."

"I'm not allowed to say 'my goodness,'" Gia said.

Zac leaned over and said quietly, "You don't correct adults, Gia. And you keep forgetting that you don't talk at the table unless someone speaks directly to you."

Have I said something wrong? Jane wondered what was wrong with what she'd said. Now she would have to be careful, not only to be mindful of cursing, but anything else that the Amish wouldn't normally say—especially with a child around. "I'm sorry if I said something wrong."

"It doesn't matter. I'm the one who's sorry. Gia isn't used to being around... she's not used to being here at the B&B with a lot of people." Zac gave Jane a smile, which seemed sincere.

Jane knew that Zac meant that Gia hadn't spent much time around *Englischers,* which were what the Amish called people like her.

"You don't have to eat it if you don't want to," Mrs. Yoder said to Jane regarding the food.

"Oh." Jane gave a little laugh. "I love apple pie. I'm sure I can squeeze some in."

Sarah cut the pie and passed Jane a piece, after

generous dollops of cream and ice-cream had been added.

"I made the ice-cream," Mrs. Yoder said. "The girls made the apple pie."

Jane waited until everyone had dessert in front of them before she started. "Mmm, it's delicious—all of it."

"Thank you," Lizzie said.

"Tell me what plans you have for the place and how it's going to be different than it was before," Jane said, hoping her mind could be kept busy and away from her late husband.

Lizzie said, "We're making the rooms better and adding more en-suites. People don't like having to leave their rooms and go down the hallway to shower."

Zac added, "After we get the house renovated, I suggested to have some self-contained cabins erected."

Lizzie nodded. "That's some time away, if we do well after the renovations. Seems everyone who comes to stay wants everything self-contained, their own bathroom, and a small tea and coffee making area with a small fridge. Not everyone wants to join us for dinner."

Tobias chimed in, "Some have dinner with us some nights, but then want to experience some of the restaurants around town and about the place."

Lizzie said to her husband, "She asked about the B&B, Tobias."

He motioned with his hands about a yard apart.

"I'm trying to give her the broad view of things. You mentioned the dinner."

Lizzie turned back to her. "Does that answer your question, Jane?"

"Yes, you're giving people what they want, which is great. And people like their own private bathroom. When was the Rose Room renovated?"

"I did that one a couple of years ago," Zac said.

Jane looked at Zac. "And you and Gia live here too?"

He nodded. "We moved back recently."

"It's certainly a huge house."

"It's been added onto over the years," Zac said.

Gia yawned a big yawn.

"Looks like it's close to someone's bedtime," Tobias said smiling at Gia.

"I'm not tired." Gia frowned.

CHAPTER 5

Let no man despise thy youth;
but be thou an example of the believers,
in word, in conversation, in charity,
in spirit, in faith, in purity.
1 Timothy 4:12

AFTER DINNER, Jane went back to her room. It'd been awhile since she'd had a lovely home-cooked meal like the one she'd just had. She had to admit that she liked the whole Yoder family—although Zac seemed to have a chip on his shoulder.

Jane grabbed the robe behind the door and headed for the shower. Even though she normally preferred to relax in the tub, tonight she was so tired she didn't want to run the risk of falling asleep in the bathtub.

"If I drowned in the bathtub, all Derek's dreams would come true. I'm not going to give him that satisfaction." There were only two reasons to continue living; one was her soon-to-be-born baby, and the other was keeping her job away from Derek. The company only had room for five account executives, and Derek had obviously seen her as the weakest person to target. The other four account executives were men.

Once the shower's hot water jets were pulsing against Jane's bare skin, she wet her hair only to realize she hadn't brought her shampoo with her. "Just my luck."

She noticed that there were small bottles of shampoo and conditioner. She picked up the shampoo and read the label to see that it was a locally sourced product based on honey. Taking the risk of what an unknown product would do to her hard-to-control hair, Jane poured a small amount of shampoo into the palm of her hand and lathered it in. Once she'd rinsed, she applied the conditioner, pleased with its smell. After she had waited to let the conditioner do its work, she closed her eyes tightly and let the warm water flow over her whole body washing away every trace.

At the same time, Jane tried hard to visualize all her problems heading down the drain with the water. It worked for a couple of minutes, but then she reminded herself to call the life insurance company and make that claim. Back to the task of letting her problems go. She again pushed aside all worries, and all the things that still needed to be done, to imagine sitting under a waterfall, alone, with no worries and nothing that needed to be done.

Like they usually did, one thought came into her head, bringing another and then another. It was the insurance company call that she was now dwelling on. One bright spot in all she'd been through was that Sean had bought life insurance.

Jane stepped out of the shower and dried herself briskly with a white fluffy towel before she pulled on the robe and left the bathroom. Realizing her phone hadn't rung all day, she fished it out of her bag wondering if the battery had gone dead.

It was on. Jane looked closely at the screen to read, "No service!" She'd have to use the phone in the reception area tomorrow to make some calls. Although she didn't have the life insurance policy number with her, surely they could look up the details from their end to get the claim underway.

She fished her hair dryer out of the drawer where she'd only just placed it, wondering how she could forget her shampoo and conditioner but remember her dryer and flat iron. As her naturally-curly hair was always frizzy, as soon as it was dry she always straightened it.

Back in the bathroom, she plugged the dryer in, remembering that her mother told her never to wash her hair at night. Her mother had died in a car accident when Jane was nineteen and she'd been on her own until she'd met Sean. It was odd that Sean would die in the same way as her mother had. Now she was well and truly on her own with no family, having no idea who or where her father was. Most of her friends were from work, and now that they hadn't alerted her to what Derek was up to, she questioned their friendship.

When her hair was finally straight, Jane plastered night-cream on her face, exchanged the robe for her nightgown, grabbed one of the books she'd brought with her, and finally headed for bed. She hadn't gotten two pages in when she fell asleep.

∽

THE NEXT MORNING, Jane walked into the dining room to see only Gia and Zac sitting at the table.

No sooner had she sat down than Zac leaned toward her. "I'm sorry if I was rude last night. It seems we might have gotten off to a bad start."

"I didn't notice," Jane said. Realizing that she might have sounded rude when he was offering an apology, she added, "All forgiven."

"If you'd like, I can show you around and give you some history of the place this morning."

"What about all the work you've got to do?"

Zac smiled. "I can't do anything until I get a delivery which is expected around lunch time. So, I have the time."

"I'd love that, thank you. The only thing is that I've got a few calls to make."

"How about if I come back around ten?"

"That would be perfect."

He poured Jane a cup of tea and pushed it forward to her.

"Thank you."

"Can I come, *Dat?*" Gia asked.

"It's *schul* for you today."

"Again?"

"*Jah,* again."

"I don't wanna go. I wanna stay here with you."

Zac said to his daughter, "You need to know things and *schul* will teach you these things."

She hung onto her father's hand and looked up at him. "You could teach me."

"I could, but I've got things to do for *grossdaddi* and *grossmammi.*"

"Okay."

He looked over at Jane. "I'll be back at ten."

"Okay, see you then," she said, pleased to have something to occupy herself with. "Then I might spend the rest of the day reading. Tomorrow I might have a look around town and see what there is to see." She took another mouthful of tea.

"My mother can tell you about what there is to do and see."

"What will I do?"

They looked around to see Lizzie walking into the room.

Zac said, "I was just telling Jane that you'd be able to tell her what there is to do around here."

"Yes, I'll go through it with you later today. I've got lots of brochures of different places you can visit. I'll dig them out. I put them away when I thought we'd be closed to the public." Lizzie gave a good-hearted chuckle.

"Before my work colleague talked you into having me?"

"Yes. He was such a lovely man. He wouldn't take 'no' for an answer. I wonder why he particularly wanted you to stay here?"

"It's hard to tell with him, but he would've had some kind of a reason he wanted me here. He's an enigma."

"What's..." Gia began before her father raised his hand to silence her.

"Remember what I told you about talking at the table?"

"It's hard for me to remember that, *Dat,* when everyone else is talking."

"Everyone else is an adult and you're a child. If we're to eat here with other guests when they come, they aren't going to want to talk with a child all the time."

Gia looked upset and Jane felt so sorry for her.

"Were you going to ask me what an enigma is, Gia?"

Gia nodded.

"An enigma is someone who is hard to understand —someone who is a little odd."

Gia smiled and nodded as though she understood.

"Thank you for explaining that to her, Jane."

Jane looked across at Zac, wondering if she'd undermined his authority by answering Gia's question. By his sincere smile, she knew she hadn't.

Once the girls came in with a breakfast of eggs, bacon, sausages and fried tomatoes, Jane asked, "Where is Mr. Yoder this morning?"

"He's not one for breakfast. He wakes up later in the day. You see, he stays up very late at night, and so he wakes up late too."

"He must be a night owl," Jane said.

Gia covered her mouth and giggled.

Jane and Zac looked at each other and exchanged smiles. Whatever aggravation there had been yesterday between Zac and herself, it seemed to be eroding.

"The breakfast was amazing, Lizzie," Jane said when she'd finished.

Lizzie said, "Thank you. More hot tea?"

"No thanks. I've had more than enough of everything."

"If you'll excuse me, I'll have to get Gia off to school. And I'll see you at ten, Jane."

When Zac left with Gia, Jane asked if she could use

the phone in the reception area. Once she'd gotten the calls out of the way, she'd be able to relax.

As Jane left the dining room, she wondered if she should suggest to the Yoders that they have phones in each of the guest rooms. Perhaps that would be too much trouble for them and create more work. It was possible that the people who stayed so far away from everything didn't want to be bothered by phones. And now that so many people had cell phones, it wasn't worth considering.

Jane fetched a pen and notebook from her room and headed to the phone. Picking up the receiver, she leaned against the reception desk and dialed her work number. As soon as she told Trudy, the receptionist, who she was, she was hung up on.

That's strange! She hung up on me. No, we must've been cut off.

She dialed the number again, thinking it must've been a mistake, but when the same thing happened again, she knew she'd have to call Tyrone directly. She'd been trying to get the gossip of what was going on from Trudy, and now Jane was truly worried about what was happening in her absence.

"This is Tyrone."

"It's me—Jane."

"Why are you calling? You're supposed to be having time off; and that means no contact with work."

"I just called Trudy and she hung up on me—twice."

"That's under my orders. If you call anybody who

works here, that's the response you'll get. Under my instructions, they're going to end the call immediately."

"That's hardly fair."

"You're not being fair to yourself. Why do you think I've gone to all this trouble to get you to rest? It's a paid vacation. Enjoy it!"

"I thank you for that, but you know I can't relax and I'm not good at taking vacations."

"You'll have to learn, or what good are you going to be to the company?"

"What do you mean? I'm just worried that Derek might need help with the O'Connor account that I brought in. And I'm not so sure he's the right person to look after the other accounts while I'm gone either. I didn't have time to tell the board of directors at O'Connor and Gamble that I'd be gone for a few weeks. Have you called them yet?"

"Derek met with them yesterday."

"What?" she shrieked.

"I said Derek had a meeting with them yesterday."

"I heard what you said. I'm shocked. How could he have possibly arranged that so quickly?"

"It's under control. Calm down. This business has to run without you."

"Am I fired?"

Tyrone laughed. "No, of course not. You can't be here all the time, though, especially not when you have the baby. Have you given thought to how drastically you'll have to change things here?"

"I'll manage, just like I've always managed. I am worried about Derek's experience."

"He's doing fine."

"With what? He wouldn't have had time to do anything to be 'fine' at. Except have that meeting with them, I suppose. I don't know how he pulled that off so quickly."

"Stop worrying! That's why I told everyone to hang up on you. And also your cell has been canceled."

"What?"

"Canceled."

"I thought it was out of range. You mean I can't call out?"

"That's right."

"You cut it off? I need the phone; I'm pregnant if you hadn't noticed. What if I have an emergency and need to use it?"

"Derek checked that when he suggested to cancel it. It's enabled for 911 calls, but that's all."

"It was Derek's idea?" She stamped her foot trying her best to stop herself from screaming. From that point on, the brakes were off. "Can't you see that Derek has cooked up this whole scheme? He knows I hate the Amish and where does he send me? He's been scheming to get my job from the beginning."

There was silence on the other end of the phone; she knew she'd made a huge mistake by yelling at her boss and letting him know what she thought of Derek. This was exactly the reaction Derek would've wanted her to have. Her rant would be blamed on pregnancy hormones and that would be the next reason to keep her away from work.

"See how much you need this vacation? You're being paranoid."

"That's it. I'm coming back today, Tyrone. I'm not going to put up with being put in a box like Derek's trying to do. I can't relax here. I need to be working!"

"No! I'm your boss and I'm giving you a direct order. You are not coming back here until your vacation is over with. If you do, I'll have security escort you off the premises."

"I thought we were friends."

"As your friend, I'm giving you the best advice I can, and that is to take a break— have this vacation and enjoy it." After Jane didn't speak, Tyrone added, "Look, why don't I pop down and see you in a couple of weeks?"

She nodded.

"Are you still there? Or have you hung up on me?"

"I nodded," Jane said wiping a tear from her right eye.

"Go and do something relaxing and I'll see you in a couple of weeks."

Tyrone ended the call.

It wasn't good that Tyrone had so much confidence in the sneaky Derek.

Knowing there wasn't much she could do about Tyrone and Derek, she looked down at the next phone number on the list—the life insurance company.

She knew she'd sounded like a crazy person on the phone, but Tyrone needed to see what Derek was really like.

After speaking for fifteen minutes with the woman at the claims department of the life insurance company, Jane still couldn't take in what the representative had told her. Sean had canceled his life insurance six months before he died. From what she understood, he'd cashed in the policy, and had gotten $30,000 from it. Where had the cash gone? It certainly hadn't landed in their joint account. Now she'd have to phone the lawyer to see if he could trace the money. But not today

Now she had nothing—no life insurance money and nothing for the future of her child. All her hopes of paying off the mortgage had come to nothing. She hung up the phone and looked around, hoping no one had overheard what she was saying.

"Oh, I'm sorry, dear, are you finished with the phone?"

Everything faded around Jane and then she was engulfed in darkness. When she came to, she saw two fuzzy figures leaning over her. At first she didn't know where she was, and then she remembered she was with the Amish on a forced vacation. She tried to sit up, but when she remembered what Tyrone had said about Derek suggesting to cut off her phone, and what she'd found out about the life insurance money she was never going to get, all strength left her and she lay back down.

"Are you alright?" Lizzie asked while tapping on her hand.

"Yes, I think so. Did I faint?" She looked at the other person leaning over her to see that it was Tobias.

"Let's get her over to the couch, Tobias."

"Are you alright to stand?" Tobias asked.

She shook her head. "I don't think so. Not just yet; I need to stay here awhile."

"A glass of water! Quick!" Lizzie ordered Tobias. While he was gone, Lizzie asked, "How far along are you?"

"Six months."

"And have you had fainting spells before?"

"No, never. Do you think I have something—that something's wrong with the baby?"

"I don't know, but I have a friend who's a midwife and she'd be able to check you over and make sure everything's okay."

"Yes, yes please; that would be good. I have had all the tests and there was nothing wrong before. I hope nothing's gone wrong." All strength had left her body, so much so that she found it an effort even to speak.

"Don't worry about it. I'm sure your baby's fine," Lizzie said before she stood and took a couple of steps towards the phone. "I'll call her now."

"Thank you."

While Lizzie made the call, Jane hoped it was only the nasty couple of shocks she'd gotten that caused her to faint.

Lizzie got off the phone just as Tobias handed Jane a glass of water.

"Can you sit up?" Tobias took the glass back and held it for her while she sat up.

"I spoke to my friend, and she's coming now," Lizzie said.

After Jane took a sip of water, she looked up at Lizzie. "That's good. Thank you. I think I can stand now."

"Help Jane to the couch, Tobias." Lizzie placed the glass on the reception desk.

With Tobias holding one arm and Lizzie the other, Jane managed to get to the couch in the reception area. She was grateful that she was the only guest; there hadn't been other guests gawking at her when she'd fainted.

CHAPTER 6

*My tongue also shall talk of thy righteousness
all the day long: for they are confounded,
for they are brought unto shame, that seek my hurt.*
Psalm 71:24

ZAC WALKED into the reception area from the rear of the house. He stared at Jane.

"Are you alright?"

His father looked up at him. "She fainted."

"She fainted?" Zac rubbed his chin while staring at Jane. "Have you called the doctor, *Mamm?*"

"I've got Gracie coming out."

He nodded. *"Gut!"*

"I'm sure I'm okay," Jane said.

"Yes, you probably are, but it doesn't hurt to have you checked over, does it? You do look pale."

Jane took a deep breath. "I suppose I am pale. I had a couple of calls with shocking news. Which I don't… I would rather not talk about."

"Yes, shock probably caused the fainting," Lizzie said.

"I can't remember that I've ever fainted before in my life."

Lizzie said, "We don't want to pry; we're just concerned for your well-being."

"Oh, Zac. You've come to show me around. I think I'll be okay to do that." She tried to stand.

"You'll do no such thing. Gracie will be here in ten minutes. She doesn't live far away; you must wait."

"Yes, I'll wait. Sorry, Zac. I'm sorry. I don't know what I'm thinking. Of course I'll wait for her."

Zac walked closer. "Whatever disturbed you in those phone calls, for the sake of your baby you must not let it upset you." His voice trailed off at the end.

Once she saw the concern in his face, she nodded. "I'll try not to worry."

But not worrying was easier said than done. A few seconds later, all she could think of was how much more important it was that she keep her job now that there was no life insurance money coming her way. She couldn't explain that to the Amish, who were religious and didn't care about possessions or sending their children to good schools. They wouldn't know what it was like to live in a dog-eat-dog world. She'd overcome so many obstacles as a woman to get where she was, and she couldn't let Derek take it all away from her now.

"I hope everything will be okay."

Jane buried her thoughts as she looked into Zac's comforting brown eyes, which were staring into hers; she was sure they'd just shared a moment. Her ego needed that little boost after having her late husband leave her for another woman. "Thank you."

"I'll leave you in my mother's hands and I'll see you a little later."

"At lunchtime. Don't be late!" Lizzie said to Zac.

"Yes, at lunch." Jane stared after Zac as he walked out the door. Maybe she'd hit her head when she'd fallen; Zac certainly seemed more handsome than he had yesterday when she'd met him.

At the sound of a car outside, Lizzie looked out the door. "That's her now."

"She's not Amish?" Jane had expected an Amish midwife to arrive in a buggy, not a car. Or maybe the midwife wasn't Amish at all.

"She takes a taxi when she's in a hurry. We're allowed to ride in cars, but we mustn't drive them ourselves."

"Yes, I knew that about the driving cars," Jane said.

The midwife came in carrying a large bag. She was a woman of around fifty with pale skin, blue eyes and a pretty smile. She looked small against Lizzie Yoder's large frame.

"This is our patient, Gracie." Mrs. Yoder introduced the two women.

"Hello, and goodbye, Gracie," Tobias said. "You don't need me around."

Gracie giggled. *"Nee,* we don't need you right now, Tobias."

When Tobias was out of the room, Jane said, "I was explaining to Lizzie that I've been checked over fully. I've had two ultrasounds already, and my blood work was fine."

Gracie nodded and proceeded to pull things out of her bag.

Jane licked her lips. "Before I fainted, I had a nasty couple of surprises."

"Yes, she had two phone calls that upset her," Lizzie explained.

"Would that have made me faint?" Jane asked Gracie.

Gracie raised her eyebrows. "Yes, shock can do that, but I'll check you over to be on the side of safety."

As Jane was having her blood pressure taken, she wondered how experienced the woman was. "Do you deliver a lot of babies around here?"

"Yes I do, but it might not sound like many to you. This year, I've been busy with twenty eight babies, but the year before it was twenty. I cover most of the local counties."

"That seems a lot to me. Are they all home births?"

"Mostly home births, although some women prefer

to have their babies in the hospital, and I'll go with them if they want me to. Some prefer to be in a hospital in case of emergencies."

"I've often wondered about having a homebirth. It seems to be a very natural thing to do."

"I agree. To my way of thinking, hospitals are for sick people not for women having babies. I'm afraid the culture is leaning more and more toward..." Gracie laughed. "You don't want to listen to me prattle on about births."

"I do. I'm very interested."

"Let me say just this—modern ways are good for when things go wrong, but when things aren't going wrong, it's best for a birth to go naturally."

Jane said, "I've read a lot about birthing over the years, and I've read that lying flat on one's back is not the ideal position to give birth."

Gracie frowned and shook her head. "No. It's best to squat as that gives a greater opening for the baby's head to move through. Many hospitals aren't designed to provide for that except for ones with birthing centers."

"I wish you were closer to New York. I'd love to have a birth at home."

"Is that where you live?" Gracie asked.

Jane nodded.

"Well, your blood pressure is normal, although a little on the low side. But that would be expected with your dizzy spell."

"My blood pressure has always been good."

Gracie said, "Surely there'd be midwives in New York willing to do home births?"

"I haven't really had the time to inquire. I guess there would have to be."

"How long are you going to leave it?" Lizzie butted in.

"I know I need to do it. It's just another thing on my list."

"That should be on the very top of your list," Lizzie said.

"I've just had been preoccupied with other things." She felt comfortable enough with Lizzie and Gracie to admit, "My husband died just recently. And I love my job, but it's pretty intense. I've been under a lot of stress."

"I'm sorry," Gracie said.

Lizzie pressed her lips together and nodded in agreement with Gracie.

"I don't talk about myself to people very much. I've always been a bit of a loner and that's probably because I'm an only child."

"How long are you here for?" Gracie asked.

Lizzie answered for her, "Jane is here for four weeks. Her boss made her take four weeks off and made her come here."

"I hope to see more of you and we can talk about births. Is this your first?" Gracie asked.

"Yes, it is."

"I thought so."

"I'd really like to talk with you some more. And I'd really like to know more about the pros and cons of having a homebirth. It's something that I always thought I would do if I ever had a child."

"Why don't we make a time right now? I'm pretty well booked up this week. What about some time next week?"

"That sounds wonderful. I'll fit in with whatever time suits you. I really do need to get things organized because once I get back to work…"

"Work? You'll be seven months gone when you leave here. Are you going back to work?" Lizzie asked.

"Don't women work in the fields right up to giving birth and then they continue on after the birth?" Jane asked.

Lizzie laughed. "Who are these people you're speaking of?"

"Every mother needs a little rest and to be taken care of," Gracie said.

Who will care for me? I have no one. Jane had no family and her only friends were fair-weather friends, it seemed, by the way Trudy hung up on her so cruelly.

"How about I come by next week on Tuesday?"

"That sounds truly wonderful. Thank you very much. I'll really look forward to it."

"Now take it easy and rest." Gracie packed her bag. "Just no more stress." She wagged a finger in her face.

Lizzie said, "I'm going to take you under my wing,

young lady, and see to it that you don't have any stress while you're here."

Jane nodded at Lizzie who reminded her a little of her late mother.

"Why don't you go and have a rest, and I'll knock on your door when lunch is ready. If you don't feel you can make it to the dining room, I'll bring a tray to your room."

"Thank you. I'll be okay to come to the dining room. I'm feeling better now, but a rest does sound good."

"Come on." Lizzie offered her hand. "I'll escort you to your room."

Jane said goodbye to Gracie and headed to her room.

CHAPTER 7

*For the which cause I also suffer these things:
nevertheless I am not ashamed: for I know whom I have
believed,
and am persuaded that he is able to keep that which I have
committed unto him against that day.*
2 Timothy 1:12

ONCE JANE WAS in the warm bed of the B&B, she closed her eyes and tried to push her troubles aside. Her baby kicked, and she covered her belly with her hands. "It's okay, baby. We'll get through all our hard times and we'll have a wonderful life—just you and me conquering the world together."

It didn't take long before sleep overtook her.

The next thing she was aware of was a gentle knock

on her door. "Are you awake, Jane?" It was Lizzie.

"Yes. I'll be out in a minute. Thank you." She assumed that lunch was ready. A quick glance at the bedside clock told her it was one in the afternoon. Jane sat up slowly in case she was still suffering from dizziness. When she felt fine, she slowly stood. After she straightened herself up, and put on a little lipstick, she made her way to the dining room.

The first person she saw was Zac, who jumped to his feet when she entered the room. "How are you feeling now?" he asked.

"I'm a lot better. I really feel fine, thank you." She sat down next to Lizzie where she'd sat the previous day.

"That's good," Lizzie said, "And after a good meal you'll feel even better."

"Are you still able to show me around today, Zac? Would you have time?"

He nodded. "They called to say the delivery is going to be delayed. I'll make time, as long as you're sure you're up to it."

"I am."

~

When their lunch was over, Zac said to Jane, "Come along; forget those troubling calls and I'll show you around the place." When they walked through the back door of the living room Zac offered his arm. She looped her arm through his and they walked along the outside of the house.

He pointed to the section made out of rock. "The original house is everything you can see that's made out of river rock."

Jane looked up at the whitish gray stones that made up the building.

"After the original owners' children were born—all fifteen of them, they needed more room and built on this area here. It was once bedrooms, but we turned it into the kitchen and the dining room."

"And these were your ancestors through your father's line?"

"That's right. My father and his father built the rest of the house. It was my grandfather who first opened the house to paying guests. That was before there was any electricity to the house."

"So you're both builders? Both you and your father?"

He shook his head. "Building is something most every Amish man learns to do. My father was a farmer who did a lot of building—so I guess you could say he's a builder."

"He's done a very good job of it. It certainly looks like it was all built at the one time. Nothing looks added on. Except for the original stone house."

He chuckled. "While I've got you alone I just wanted to say I hope you don't think I'm being too hard on Gia."

"Not at all. In what way do you mean?"

"My parents aren't used to children talking at the dinner table; that's how we were raised. I'm the youngest of six boys. They never allowed us to speak at the table, and out of respect for them, I try not to allow Gia to speak at the table."

"That makes sense. I think you're lovely to Gia."

He smiled at her. "I like chatting with Gia over dinner, and my wife and I... we used to all talk with each other."

"I hadn't really thought about it too much. I think it's an old-fashioned thing. I remember my grandmother saying she wasn't allowed to speak at the table."

They continued walking while he pointed out more things around the place—the animals; the pigs, the few sheep, and a couple of milking cows.

"Can you keep going or do you want to head back?" Zac asked.

"I can walk further."

"Are you sure? I don't want to wear you out."

"I'm fine," Jane insisted.

He looked down at her and smiled. His smile turned into a good-natured laugh. "You seem quite different from the woman who showed up here yesterday."

"This is the relaxed me. The woman who showed up yesterday was the tense and stressed me. Apart from that, I was a little shocked when I arrived at an Amish place. It was all arranged for me by my work.

There's this one man at work who's trying to take over my job."

Zac threw his head back and laughed. When she didn't laugh with him, he stopped. "Oh, you're serious?"

"Quite serious! He forced me away and now he's taking over everything. And I can't do anything about it because he's got a hold of my boss' ear. My boss, Tyrone, has ordered everyone to hang up on me when I call."

He nodded. "Is that what caused you to faint?"

She nodded. "Yes, and right after that, I found out my late husband canceled his life insurance policy. I was expecting money for my child's future and now it's not going to come through."

"That's dreadful."

She stared at him, and saw he seemed overly concerned. "Don't worry, my stay here is all paid for."

"I'm not concerned about that. In your condition, you'd want to feel secure wouldn't you?"

"That's exactly right. I'd want to feel secure, and now I feel anything but secure."

"I'm sorry, and I hope I didn't make you feel worse."

"Don't worry; nothing could make me feel worse than I already do."

He blew out a deep breath. "I guess we all have our burdens to bear."

On glancing up at his frowning face, Jane knew he carried his own private pain. It couldn't be easy for him to move back in with his parents and be raising Gia on his own, without his wife.

"I'm sorry. I'm very selfish talking about myself all the time. I'm sure you've got your own problems. It can't be easy for you now that your wife has gone."

"I'm blessed that I have my parents who do most of the work looking after Gia. My brothers are all married and I guess if I didn't have my parents, my brothers' families would all help out."

"Yes I've read about the Amish. I used to have a fascination for the Amish and I really liked reading about them."

He smiled at her. "Is that so? What did you learn about us?"

"You have a community spirit and you're all there to help one another. You'll take care of one another—offer a helping hand if someone has fallen and needs help to get back up."

Zac nodded. "That is what it's like; we do help one another."

As they walked few more paces in silence, fearful thoughts of how alone she truly was, ran through her head once again.

"Do your parents live close to where you live?"

She shook her head. "I never knew my father, and my mother died some years ago."

"I'm sorry. I shouldn't have asked."

"That's okay. I don't mind talking about them. My baby and I will be pretty much on our own."

"No brothers or sisters?"

"I'm an only child. My father was gone before I was born, and my mother worked constantly and never remarried."

He nodded. "Gia has many cousins around her age—she's blessed in that regard."

"That's really good. She's a lovely little girl."

He smiled. "I think so. Can you walk to those trees over there?" He nodded his head toward a clump of bushes.

"Yes."

"I'll show you where my forefathers got the stones to build the house."

"From the river?"

He nodded. "From the river and the surrounds."

"I'd love to take a look."

As she walked quietly alongside the handsome Amish man, she realized that this man wanted nothing from her except her company. He had nothing to sell her, he was not trying to date her, and neither was he trying to profit from her nor take what was hers. It was a refreshing change to be with a person who had no agenda.

"That's better," he said.

"What's that?"

"It's nice to see you smile."

"I tend to do that accidentally from time to time."

He laughed. "Not too often from what I've seen."

"I'll do what I can to change that. I don't want to be

stressed and on edge anymore. There are obviously a few things in my life I need to change."

"I'm sure you'll figure things out."

"I will." She looked down. "Oh, the rocks! They're the same as the ones in the house."

He nodded. "They are. There was once a path built alongside the riverbank. It was a walking trail. It's grown over long ago. I've always wanted to restore it, but there's always something else to do."

"Like the renovations?"

"Yes. And since Gia and I have moved back here, I kind of have to do what my parents want me to do."

"That's not such a bad problem to have."

"I know, but I do feel I'm being watched over, much like I'm a child again myself."

"I suppose that's only normal. I'd feel like that if I was living with my parents, if they were still alive that is." They walked a few more steps alongside the river. "Gia's an unusual name; that's not Amish is it?"

He shook his head. "No. It was my wife's idea to call her that. I wanted to call her Maize. My wife wasn't a traditional kind of woman."

Jane raised her eyebrows. "I would've gone with Gia too."

Zac frowned. "Don't be like that. Maize was my favorite aunt. She was my father's sister; she died when I was ten. Aunt Maize and I just seemed to click."

Jane laughed with him and was surprised how

comfortable she felt with him. "It's so beautiful here. Maybe they were right to make me take a vacation."

"There's a time for work and a time for rest and I'd say that you're most certainly in a place where you need a rest." He looked down at her. "Why don't we sit down?"

"Do I look like I'm going to fall, or something?"

"You are a bit pale. I wouldn't want to be held responsible for you fainting again." He nodded at something over her right shoulder.

She looked around to see a stone bench. Turning back to him, she said, "Did you put that there just for me?"

"I did. Just before lunch. I carved it out of one rock because I knew you'd need to sit down.

Jane gave a small laugh as he guided her to the whitish-gray stone seat.

They sat down and looked out across the river.

"I'm sorry I told you so much about myself. That's something I never really do. I don't know why it's easier sometimes to talk with someone you don't know."

"I'm happy to listen. As I said, I've had my fair share of pain."

"I hope you don't mind me asking, but how did your wife die?"

He looked down at the palms of his hands for a moment and then looked over across the river. "I haven't talked about it much." He grimaced. "That's something we have in common—not talking too much. She was killed in an accident."

She shook her head and looked at Zac. "I'm sorry about your wife. My husband died in a car accident."

"She left me a note saying she was leaving me."

"No!" His story was similar to her own. She shook her head in sorrow. "Since I've already told you half of my life story, I might as well tell you the rest. The night he died, my husband announced that he was leaving me for another woman. He'd been carrying on an affair with her for a whole year. He blamed me; can you believe it? He blamed me for him leaving because I was 'so consumed with work that I didn't have time for him.'"

He gave a nod. "I'm sorry to hear that. The strange thing is that my wife died in the exact same way. She was leaving me to be with an *Englischer*."

She shook her head. "It taints their memory. Well, it taints my memory of Sean."

"Sean?" he jumped up.

She frowned. "Yes, his name was Sean."

"Please tell me it wasn't Sean Fordyce."

Her jaw dropped open and she had no words. She stared at him and nodded.

He sat down, and said in a low voice, "Isn't your name Walker?"

"I go by my maiden name—Walker. I never took Sean's name. So it was your wife he was running away with?"

"It seems so. That was the man's name on the note she left." He lowered his head and rubbed his forehead with the palms of his hands. "I didn't know the affair had been going on for a year."

"I'm sorry."

He sat up straight. "There's nothing for you to be sorry for."

Then it suddenly made perfect sense to Jane. Derek had set this whole thing up. He must've found out that Sean had crashed the car with a woman in the passenger seat who also died. His research must've led him to Zac Yoder and the B&B.

"Zac, I think that someone at work sent me here on purpose. Derek must've found out that Sean was in the car with your wife at the time of the accident."

"Why would he do that?"

"To upset me. He really is trying to take my place at work."

"Well, we both mustn't let it upset us, then. Neither of us had any part in our spouses' decisions. It was their choice to leave us."

Jane looked into his brown eyes. No woman in her right mind would surely ever leave him, but Jane knew she hadn't been a good wife to Sean.

"You're looking at me like you think the accident was your fault."

"If I had been a better wife, he wouldn't have had an affair. I let him down so many times. I wouldn't take his last name because I was known professionally as

Jane Walker, and I delayed having children." She blinked back tears, wondering if Sean would've left if he'd known she was expecting a child. She'd delayed telling him because he would've insisted she leave work, whereas she wanted to keep working.

"None of this is your fault. You were even giving him a child."

"That's true," she said through sniffs. "But I hadn't told him about the baby. I don't know why. I guess I should've told him as soon as I found out." What she didn't tell Zac was that she'd told Sean she never wanted children. She knew she wasn't going to be a good mother, but now that a child was on the way, she was determined to be the very best mother she could.

"A child is a blessing. You'll find that out."

She smiled at the look in his eyes as he spoke about children. Then she shook her head as Derek popped into her mind. "I can't believe Derek would do this."

"Is Derek the man from work?"

She nodded.

"If he's done this to upset you, don't let it. You and I will form a friendship, an alliance and be strong together." He put his large hand out, palm facing up.

She placed her hand in his and he closed his fingers and gave her hand a squeeze as he smiled. Embarrassed to touch a stranger in such a way, she pulled her hand back.

"Maybe you should tell someone at work what Derek has done," he said.

"I would look silly, and besides, I don't think Tyrone would believe Derek did it deliberately. They would say my pregnancy hormones were making me paranoid."

"And are they?"

She laughed. "Obviously not! Well, maybe in some way they're making me mad, but not paranoid."

"I think you're doing remarkably well. I've got a daughter to raise on my own, but I've got family helping me. You've got to get through the birth, find your way after the baby's born, and work a job as well."

She shook her head. "Don't talk about it. It's all too much for me to think about right now."

"You'll get through it. From what I've seen, you're a strong woman."

"I've had to fight many battles to get where I am in my career." When he raised his eyebrows, she smiled. "Not fight physically, of course, but I've had a lot of obstacles put in my way from people like Derek."

"Maybe you weren't sent here by Derek, maybe you were sent here by someone else, so you and I could meet and help one another."

Jane smiled and looked over the water. "You mean, sent from God?"

"Yes."

She giggled. "That's nice of you to say. It makes me feel better thinking there's a higher power at work rather than that I'm being manipulated by Derek."

"Go ahead and think that way, then."

"I shall. I feel better already."

He gave a sharp nod. "Good!"

"Do your parents know your wife had left you—and all that?"

"They do. Everyone in the community knows she was leaving me. Many of them say the car accident was God's judgment on her."

Jane was surprised, thinking it seemed a little judgmental. "Is that what you think?"

He shook his head. "I think God judges us on the great judgment day. I don't think He punishes us and makes bad things happen while we're here."

Jane sighed. She was trying to get by in this life rather than thinking about what was going to happen after. "I guess I couldn't take it all in at the time—to recall her name even if they'd told me. All I remember was that they said she was an Amish woman and was wearing Amish clothes. After he was gone, I saw from his credit card statement that he'd shopped at a women's clothing store. I guess he'd bought her some clothes to change into, but they never got that far." She looked back at him to see him staring at the ground. "I'm sorry. I shouldn't be talking about these things."

He shook his head. "I'm still getting used to everything. Maybe—I'm not sure what it is."

"It's beautiful here by the river."

"It is. It's my favorite place to be. I do feel dreadful that my wife caused you so much pain."

"You couldn't help it. I don't blame anyone."

"Now, that's three shocks you've had today. Will

you be okay to walk back?"

"Yes, I will." She looked into his eyes. "I'm glad I came here. I feel better about things now."

He nodded. "Me too."

They walked back to the house in silence as Jane wondered whether she should tell Tyrone about the game that Derek was playing. She ran the risk of Tyrone not believing a word she said, and that was the reason that stopped her from calling him again.

Taking a sideways glance at Zac, she wondered why his wife would've decided to leave him, and why she had felt the need to carry on a secret affair. Jane was tempted to ask Zac if he knew where his wife had met Sean, but Zac had already shared enough with her for one day. Perhaps they'd talk about it some more over the next few weeks. She already felt better finding out that another human understood her pain— almost as though she'd found a kindred spirit within Zac, who shared her pain. He surely knew part of what she'd been going through. Not only had she lost a spouse, the loss came directly after the confession of the greatest deception anyone could experience.

"You doing okay?" he asked.

She smiled at him and nodded. "I am. I suppose I'll just spend the rest of the day resting and reading. Thank you for showing me around the place."

"I didn't show you much. I hope you'll allow me to give you another tour another day?"

"I'd like that."

He pushed the back door of the house open and she walked in, wondering if he would follow. She turned around when he stayed on the step.

"I'll get back to work," he said as he glanced behind him. "That's the delivery truck now."

∽

"How are you doing now?" Lizzie asked when Jane walked into the common room.

"I'm feeling much better now after that walk in the fresh air."

"That's good. And I hope you put your worries to rest at least for now."

"Yes I have. Talking with Zac helped."

Lizzie looked at her as though she were startled. "Talking with Zac helped?"

"Yes." Jane didn't know what Lizzie's reaction would have been if she'd told her that Zac's wife had been running away with her husband when she'd been killed. It wasn't her information to tell. "I think I might lie down in my room and read."

"Good idea! I'll come and get you when dinner is ready if you like. You're always welcome to sit and read here in the sunroom, too. Guests come in here all the time."

"Thank you, I might do that later. I think I'll just read in bed for now, and I might be able to fall asleep for a little while."

Lizzie nodded. "I'll come and fetch you for dinner if you're not in the dining room by then."

"Thank you. I wouldn't want to miss out on dinner." She walked out of the sunroom and headed to her bedroom—the Rose Room.

Once in her room, she recovered her book from under the quilt and began reading from where she'd left off the night before. Although she tried her best to lose herself in the story, her thoughts returned to Zac. She wanted to learn more about him and what became of his marriage for his wife to leave him, and especially her daughter. Had Zac ignored his wife, as Sean had accused her of doing to him?

∽

"JANE."

Jane slowly opened her eyes and saw that it was dark outside. "Yes?" She pushed herself up in the bed, and the door opened.

Mrs. Yoder walked in with one of the young housemaids, who was carrying in a tray of food. "Mary has your dinner here."

"Oh, thank you. Did I sleep past dinner?"

Mary placed the tray on her nightstand.

"You did. I knocked a couple of times and when you didn't answer, I peeped in to see you fast asleep. I didn't want to wake you."

"Thank you for going to all this trouble." Jane

pushed her hair back from her face. "I didn't think I would've slept so heavily and for so long."

"You must've needed it. When you finish with your tray you can just leave it here, or put it outside your door."

Mary headed out the door in front of Lizzie.

"Thank you, Mary," Jane called after her.

The young woman turned and smiled at her.

"I would've brought the tray in myself," Lizzie said, "but I can't carry anything too heavy."

"I feel very spoiled."

"That's what vacations are about. Now, will you be needing anything else?"

"No. I'm fine." Jane knew she could make a cup of tea in the room if she needed one later.

"Good night, Jane."

"Good night, Lizzie, and thank you again."

"You're more than welcome." Lizzie smiled before she walked out of the room, closing the door behind her.

Jane leaned over and removed the lids of the containers to see what was there. There were plenty of cooked vegetables and meat with gravy. In another dish were sliced peaches with ice-cream. Not wanting to eat melted ice-cream, she did away with protocol and ate the dessert first.

Now she'd have to wait until tomorrow at breakfast to see Zac again since she'd slept past dinner.

CHAPTER 8

I have not hid thy righteousness within my heart;
I have declared thy faithfulness and thy salvation:
I have not concealed thy lovingkindness
and thy truth from the great congregation.
Psalm 40:10

JANE SAT at the dining table over a breakfast of pancakes and maple syrup.

"Do you normally have breakfast like this or only when you have guests come to stay?"

"We always have a cooked breakfast," Lizzie said.

Tobias grinned. "When we have the girls here to help."

Lizzie turned to her husband, and said, "There's only so much I can do by myself."

"Sometimes I roll my sleeves up," Tobias explained to Jane with a chuckle.

Lizzie pursed her lips. "And that's not very often, is it?"

Tobias shook his head. "I guess it isn't."

"Well, it's delicious. I haven't had pancakes like this since I don't know when."

Lizzie smiled at Jane's words.

"And what are you going to do today, Jane?" Zac asked.

"I think I'll have a quiet morning, and then this afternoon I might have a look around the town."

Zac nodded.

Jane looked at Gia, who was staring at her. "And are you going to school again today?"

"Yes, I have to; I have to go Monday through Friday. *Dat* said that I have to go. Otherwise, I wouldn't go there—ever." Gia looked up at her father. "Ms. Walker talked to me, *Dat*, or I wouldn't have spoken."

He smiled. "I noticed that; very good, Gia. Now eat up."

"You learn some good things at school, Gia," Jane said.

"That's what *Dat* keeps saying and I'm still waiting."

Tobias chuckled. "I don't think I learned anything when I was at school. Back in those days, we only went for two days a week. There were only my family and one other family of children."

"That's not helping, *Dat*," Zac said through gritted teeth.

Tobias frowned and said to Gia, "It wasn't like it is today."

"That was a very long time ago, Tobias," Lizzie said.

Zac shook his head.

Jane noticed again the age difference between Lizzie and Tobias. *I guess love knows no age,* she thought before she looked across the table at Zac. "Are you doing more of your building work today, Zac?"

"Yes, I have to get on with it. It isn't going to get finished by itself."

"Isn't it a lot of work to do alone?"

"I'm having people help out soon, but there are a few days work by myself ahead of me."

"Too bad I'm too old to help," Tobias said.

Lizzie frowned. "Well, you are, so don't go getting silly ideas into your head."

Tobias smiled like a mischievous child.

∽

WHEN BREAKFAST WAS OVER, Jane wandered to her room for her book. She would read for a couple of hours in the sunroom since it was a sunny day. After lunch, she would explore the township.

Soon after she had settled herself with a book in the sunroom, she heard noises like a horse and buggy heading to the house. She stood up and craned her neck to see that was exactly what she'd heard.

She sat back down again and found the place she'd left off reading.

A few minutes later, she noticed she wasn't alone in the sitting room. Jane looked up to see Gracie, the midwife.

"How are you feeling today, Jane?"

"Hello. I heard the buggy but didn't know it was you." Jane closed the book. "I'm feeling fine; much better today, thanks."

"It must have been the stress of those calls just like you thought. I hope whatever it was has been sorted out now."

"I don't think it can be, but I'm doing my best not to think about it."

Gracie sat next to her. "That's always best. I rearranged my appointments today because I was worried about you."

"You did that just for me?" No one had ever done anything like that for her. "That was so thoughtful. Thank you."

Gracie giggled. "I'll still come back next week to check on you. I won't do that today if you're feeling okay. Do you have plans today?"

Jane smiled and held up her book. "And this afternoon I'm going to have a look around the town."

"I could show you around."

"Could you? What about your appointments?"

"I've none today. I had two appointments that I shuffled around. I'll be happy to show you about, if you'd like."

"I'd love that."

"Good." Gracie stood up. "I'll see if Lizzie wants to come too."

Jane was pleased that she had someone to drive her and show her the township. She had a map that Lizzie had given her, but she'd never been good at reading maps.

Gracie came back into the room. "Lizzie said she won't come with us. She's got too much to do here. The girls aren't cooking lunch today, which means that you and I can have lunch in town."

"I would truly love that. Will we go now?"

"There's no reason why we can't."

"And we get to go on the buggy?"

Gracie laughed. "In the buggy—that's how we say it. Unless you'd like to walk?"

"I've never been a fan of walking. I'll just get my bag."

∽

"You look like something is on your mind, Jane. Is everything okay?"

"Well, apart from the disturbing phone calls I had yesterday I found out something else which is quite shocking."

"Do you want to tell me about it? I'm a good listener."

Looking at Gracie, she knew she could trust her. "Okay, but please, don't tell anyone. I haven't mentioned it to Lizzie."

Gracie nodded.

Jane took a deep breath. She'd gone this far and said this much; now she had to tell her what was on her mind. "I was talking to Zac yesterday. He was showing me around the B&B. Then I found out we have something very much in common."

Gracie tilted her head to one side. "What?"

"Well, I guess I'm not revealing any secrets because Zac said that everyone in the community knows that his wife was running away with another man when she was killed."

"Yes everyone knows that; you're not revealing any secrets. Go on."

"It was my husband that Zac's wife was running away with."

Gracie's jaw dropped open and she leaned back in her chair. "No!"

Jane nodded. "It's true and it is shocking. There's a man at work and he's after my job. It was he who arranged that I come to the Yoder's B&B. He must've looked into things and he made certain I was sent there."

"Why would he do that?"

"He wanted to upset me."

"That's dreadful. I'm so sorry, Jane." Gracie leaned over and touched Jane on the arm.

"I know it's rather disturbing, but still, it makes me feel better now that I've met Zac. He's going through the same thing that I'm going through—the feeling of loss and rejection."

Gracie nodded. "Zac's such a good man; he didn't deserve any of it."

"Why wasn't his wife happy with him?"

"I don't know. There wasn't any reason that I could see, but Ralene wasn't a very stable woman."

"How do you mean?" Jane asked.

She shook her head. "I shouldn't say anything."

"I'm sorry. I don't want you to betray any private information. I was just speaking in general terms."

Gracie's shoulders slumped. "Ralene didn't accept her child. When I brought Gia to her right after she was born, she yelled that it wasn't her baby. She claimed that I'd swapped Gia with another baby. But I couldn't have—there were no other babies in the house. The baby came right out of Ralene, and all I did was clear mucus away from her nose and mouth and as soon as she breathed I gave her to Ralene." Gracie shook her head. "She was a disturbed woman. And she didn't accept Gia as her daughter—it took nearly a year."

"That would've been so hard on Zac."

"It was. They never had another child."

"What do you know of their relationship?" Jane asked trying not to appear too keen to hear the answer.

"I've always been a good friend of the family and he's always been a lovely man. I've never heard a bad word about him, not even a rumour. And if he'd mistreated his wife, there would've been rumours believe me. News like that travels faster than wildfire in the community."

"Were people surprised when they learned what happened?"

"Everyone was shocked and devastated by what had happened. She left the path and she most surely must face the consequences of that on the Day of Judgment."

Jane nodded, guessing that was what the Amish thought, going by Gia's comment at the dinner table about her young friend telling her that her mother wasn't going to be with God.

"It must be hard for you to be giving birth soon and having your husband gone."

"It is. It'd be nice to have someone there for me—a partner in life. It must be hard for Zac too."

"There are a few women trying to remedy that problem." Gracie laughed.

"He has admirers?"

Gracie's eyes twinkled. "There are many women who would like to become his wife."

They were interrupted by the waitress bringing the soup they'd ordered, along with a large basket of fresh crusty bread, and butter.

Jane was determined to get the conversation away from Zac. He was starting to dominate all her thoughts. "All the food I've had since I've arrived has been truly amazing. It's only a shame I can't eat very much at one sitting."

"That's what tourists always say."

"Oh no. I hate to be one of the crowd. I've always liked to be different."

CHAPTER 9

*Now faith is the substance of things hoped for,
the evidence of things not seen.*
Hebrews 11:1

LATE THAT SAME AFTERNOON, when Jane had recovered from her day out, she headed down toward the river. She had visions of relaxing on the stone seat and watching the water ripple by. Rest and calming thoughts were what she needed right now. Not wanting to disturb Zac or have him think she wanted him to talk with her, she took a wide berth around the area of the building he'd said he was working on that day.

On her way to the river, movement to her left caught Jane's eye. She saw Zac in a paddock with a horse trotting around him in a circle. Wondering what he was doing she walked over and leaned against the top rail of the white wooden fence.

When he hadn't noticed her after a few minutes, she called out to him. "What are you doing? Aren't you supposed to be working?"

Zac looked up at her and smiled. "I have to do this. I do a bit of everything. It's all left up to me now that my parents are older." He stopped the horse.

"No. Don't let me keep you from your work. Keep going, please."

He laughed and patted the chestnut horse on his neck. "We were due to have a rest." He looked her up and down. "Where are you going to?"

"I thought I'd get back down to the river. It was peaceful there yesterday and I figured I need a bit more peace in my life."

"I think you certainly do."

"I went out with Gracie today. She took me to town, we had lunch and she showed me some places. I might go back tomorrow and have a better look around." She bit her lip hoping it didn't sound like she wanted him to offer to take her. When he nodded, she quickly asked, "What are you doing with the horse?"

"I'm training him to take a harness."

"Can you ride on his back?"

"He's too young. I got him a few months ago, but haven't had a chance to do anything with him until now."

"You can train him to pull a buggy yourself? You don't send him out somewhere to be trained?"

He shook his head. "My grandfather was a horse trainer, amongst other things. He showed me what to do."

She wanted to stay and talk with him, but at the same time, she didn't want to wear out her welcome. "I won't hold you up."

"If I wasn't in the middle of training, I'd come with you."

"That would've been nice."

"Another time?"

"I'd like that." She took a step away.

"I'll remember that," Zac said his dark eyes crinkling at the corners.

"Okay, I'll guess I'll see you at dinner?"

"Yes, I'll see you at dinner."

She looked away and before she got many steps further, she glanced over her shoulder to see he'd turned back to his horse. Not being able to stop herself, she took in the strength of his body—evident in his muscular arms—and the width of his shoulders. No wonder there were so many women who wanted to marry him. If she were Amish she'd most definitely be one of them.

Turning toward the river, Derek, work, and the O'Connor account seemed a million miles away.

Jane walked along the stones by the riverbank and imagined what it would've been like for the pioneers hundreds of years ago coming to the untamed country and making a life for themselves. Tingles ran through her body. If they could make a life for themselves out of nothing, then surely, with her strength and determination, she could rebuild hers.

Through a clearing in the trees that lined the river, Jane caught a glimpse of the house. Mentally stripping back the added on sections, she visualized the stone building as it would've been when it was first built. Jane tried to recall what Lizzie had said the first night she was there for dinner. Tobias' great-grandfather had fathered something like nineteen children.

A smile twigged Jane's lips at the thought of so many children. She thought she had problems with one on the way. The birth—she'd have to get organized soon and book into the hospital, or indeed make other arrangements if she were going to have a homebirth. Time was marching on; she'd have to decide soon.

Next week when Gracie came back to check her over, she'd make her decision after asking a lot of questions.

When the stone seat came into view, she wandered over to it and sat down. Once she was seated, she realized something that she already knew in her heart, and that was that life should be more than working seven days a week. She'd driven Sean away by her obsessiveness over work.

Jane stared at the water and pushed all thoughts out of her mind. Closing her eyes, she enjoyed the cool breeze that caressed her skin and the dappled sun kissing her skin as it shone through the trees.

∾

WHEN IT WAS time for dinner, Jane headed to the dining room. She was surprised to see only Zac and Gia sitting at the table.

"Where are your parents?" she asked Zac as she sat down.

"My mother's got a friend who's taken ill. She's gone to help look after her. My father's gone with her. They go almost everywhere together."

"I'm sorry to hear that her friend's not well. Nothing too serious I hope?"

"I'm not sure. I just got a note to say where she'd gone. I don't know anything more until she gets back."

Jane nodded and looked at Gia. "Hello, Gia."

"Hello, Ms. Walker," Gia said with a big smile on her face.

"Did you have a nice day at school?"

"It was okay," she said.

"That's good. Okay is better than horrible."

Gia giggled and covered her mouth.

"Have you lost a tooth?" Jane asked Gia

Gia nodded and took her hand away to show her. One of her middle baby teeth was missing. Jane had to stop herself from asking about the tooth fairy; she was pretty certain the Amish wouldn't have such traditions.

"You're growing up fast."

"Dat says I'm going to be tall."

The two ladies brought the dinner and placed it in the center of the table.

"I wonder what we're having tonight?" Jane said.

"I'd say chicken casserole by the smell of it." Zac pulled the lid off to reveal chicken in some kind of vegetable sauce and by the look of it, it had a lot of tomatoes.

"I'm right," he said. "I'll serve you."

"Thank you," Jane said.

Dinner went by too quickly for Jane's liking. After dinner, Zac asked if she'd like to have coffee with him in the living room after he put Gia to bed. Of course, Jane agreed.

CHAPTER 10

*While the earth remaineth, seedtime and harvest,
and cold and heat, and summer and winter,
and day and night shall not cease.*
Genesis 8:22

JANE WAITED for Zac to come into the living room, and as she waited, she read her book, trying to contain her excitement over having more time alone with him.

When he finally came into the room, he brought a tray of coffee with him.

As he poured the hot coffee into two cups, he asked, "You don't have to answer if you don't wish to, but do you know how my wife met your husband?"

Trying to hide her disappointment at him wanting to be alone with her to ask about his late wife, Jane answered, "All I know is that he traveled for his work. He must've met her in this town somewhere I'm guessing."

"It must've been hard for you with him away so much."

"I worked a lot. Looking after Sean became another chore—something else I had to do."

He raised his eyebrows. "I'd imagined you had a different relationship with your husband."

"It wasn't the kind of relationship I wanted—it never was. When I married him I thought I had a companion, someone to go through life's ups and downs with, but we never saw eye-to-eye on anything." She shook her head. "Even before we married it was like that."

"My wife," he said in a low voice, "was always unsettled. She always wanted to do different things. In the last year of her life she settled down, but that would've been when she met your husband. I guess he was consuming her attention."

"I'm sorry. I'm sorry my husband broke up your family in the way that he did."

"It's hardly your fault."

"I feel responsible. I suspected him of having affairs. I could've had him followed but I didn't. If I'd exposed him, none of this would've happened."

"We can't go back," Zac said. "And there's no use blaming yourself."

"I don't mean to. I just wish there would've been

something I could've done to stop what happened. It's a waste of two lives and it's left my child without a father and your child without a mother. It's a senseless waste."

"It was their decisions that are to blame, because of the choices they made. It's got very little to do with us."

She sniffed in an effort to stop the tears she could feel stinging behind her eyes. "I suppose you're right."

He smiled at her. "Drink your coffee it's getting cold."

She picked up the small coffee cup and took a sip. "Is your father a lot older than your mother? He appears to be."

"He's eighteen years old than she is. He'd never married and when they met, she was eighteen and he was thirty six. From the way they tell it, she was the one who approached him about marriage. He thought she was far too young for him, but she talked him 'round."

Jane laughed. "Your mother certainly seems like a woman who knows what she wants."

"She's a very strong woman. And she's gotten this B&B through some hard times. And she's made a success of it."

"Yes. It's a lovely place."

"It'll be more so when the work is done. I've got a few more days work by myself and then a team is coming to help."

"You must feel good about that." Jane had taken another sip of coffee before she realized she had given it up recently.

"I can't wait," he said with a laugh.

She placed the cup down in the saucer.

Zac asked, "Now what are you going to do about your situation at work?"

"Oh no. Don't talk about work; I'm trying to forget about it."

"Okay. I'm sorry I mentioned it," he said.

"I know you probably think I should tell my boss that Derek set me up to come here, but there's every chance my boss won't believe me and I'd look silly."

"But then there's a chance that your boss will believe you and he'll take the appropriate action."

"I kind of want to prove I'm better than Derek—do a better job than him, so if I expose him and what he's done, I might never get the chance."

"Is it important to you to prove you're better than someone else?"

"Yes. In my line of work it is. Isn't it important to everyone?"

Zac appeared to be deep in thought. "It's never bothered me that someone might be better than me at doing a certain thing."

"I live in a competitive environment, in a competitive world."

"And it creates a lot of stress for you. And that can't be healthy for you or the baby."

"You're right, but that's the way things are. Now that the insurance money isn't coming through, it makes my job even more important. And now without Sean's wages, I've only got my job to rely on."

He nodded and looked thoughtful.

Jane asked, "So what you're saying is, I should tell Tyrone what Derek has done and I shouldn't worry about proving I can do a better job than Derek? Even though I might lose my job if Derek gets what he's truly after and that is to discredit me in Tyrone's eyes."

Zac laughed. "I can't even understand what you just said; it all seems very complicated."

She bit the inside of her lip. It *was* very complicated and a simple Amish man wouldn't have the life experience to understand the complexities of corporate life. "You probably don't understand because your job is secure and you don't have to worry about money coming in or being out of work. I guess your family has relied on this B&B for a couple of generations now." She hoped she hadn't offended him.

"Yes. I suppose you're right. I wouldn't know how you feel. I've always had things I've been able to do to make money when I've needed it. That is, apart from doing work around the house. And I've got a large family of brothers and now that they've got families, their families are also mine."

"That would be nice, to have that." She rubbed her forehead with both her palms. "I think the best thing I can do is put work right out of my mind. Your mother said she wanted help with the relaunching of this place, so I'll concentrate on that." She lifted up the book that she'd brought into the room with her. "In between reading my book and seeing the sights. I'll spend a few days being a tourist."

"I'd show you around, but I have work that needs to be done."

"No. I wouldn't have you show me around; I know you're very busy. Gia seems to be adjusting well to her mother being gone."

"She's doing better now that we've moved back in with my parents and away from the house we used to live in. My wife used to leave her with other people often, and mostly with my parents. This has always been her second home."

"It makes me sad that my child will never know his, or her, father."

"It might be easier that way," Zac said, "than to lose a parent when you're old enough to know."

"Do you think so?"

He smiled back at her. "I really don't know. No child should have to be without both parents, but I think it's not something for us to question or dwell on."

"It's hard not to, but I suppose you're right because we're never going to make sense of what happened," she said knowing he probably had some religious reasons for saying what he did about not questioning.

He smiled at her and she couldn't help but smile back. "What?" she asked after a while.

"I'm pleased I've met you. I'm glad your friend sent you here. It's given me more peace."

Wanting to warm her hands, she picked up the coffee cup and wrapped both hands around it. "Me too." Jane did feel better—she felt better for meeting a man like him; a man she could talk with so easily, who understood her.

CHAPTER 11

A new commandment I give unto you, That ye love one another; as I have loved you, that ye also love one another.
John 13:33

AS SHE'D SAID she would, Gracie visited Jane the following Tuesday to check her over.

"You're in good shape and the baby's doing fine." Gracie gave Jane a hand and pulled her up to a sitting position. They were in the privacy of a small bedroom at the B&B.

"Good. That's a relief. At least something's going right in my life."

Gracie stared at her. "What's wrong?"

She shook her head. "Nothing. It's just that I feel so uncertain about the future."

"What I've learned in my fifty five years of life is that most of people's worries are about things that never actually happen."

Jane nodded. "I can't help worrying about things. It's not just my life I'm worried about, it's the baby."

"When I was a girl, my mother sat me down and said, 'Gracie, don't cross your bridges before you come to them.' That advice has been the best I've ever heard. The word of God says that worry is a useless thing. I could quote a scripture, but I won't."

"I suppose you trust in God, but I don't have a strong faith like you even though I was raised religious."

"You could still put your trust in Him. He hasn't gone anywhere."

Jane rubbed her nose. "I could try."

"Tell Him your problems and leave them with Him. Don't take them back."

Jane nodded and then Zac walked into the room.

"Oh, I'm sorry. I thought this room was vacant."

"Your *mudder* said I could use it to examine Jane."

He looked at Jane and his face flushed scarlet. "I'm sorry. I'll leave you to it."

When he closed the door, Gracie said, "Are you fond of him?"

"What do you mean?"

Gracie giggled. "Just because I've never been in love doesn't mean that I don't know it when I see it."

Jane looked down at the floor and then looked back at Gracie's smiling face. "I think I might be."

"See? You can't put anything past me."

"Nothing could ever happen between us. I don't see him changing his life and moving his daughter to New York."

"You could join us."

Jane laughed as though the idea was absurd and the thought had never occurred to her. She didn't want Gracie or anybody else to know how strongly she felt about Zac in the short time she'd known him. It hadn't been love at first sight, but maybe at second; there was an undeniable connection from her end.

"Are you okay?"

Jane nodded. "Yes. You shouldn't put those thoughts in my head, Gracie."

"I like to see others happy."

"Why have you never married?"

"It was never a decision I made. I thought somebody would turn up—everyone's got somebody, right? But no one ever showed."

"No one at all?"

"No one. I have my work to keep me happy and I love seeing babies come into the world. It's a wondrous thing to look into the eyes of a newborn." Gracie filled her lungs with air and then sighed.

"I suppose you visited other communities?"

"People visit from other communities for funerals and weddings, but with my work, I can't go too far.

There's always someone having a baby." Gracie laughed. "It's something that God didn't plan for me. I don't really think about it too much now. I've got three cats to keep me company."

"I've never had a cat."

"They're good company and they don't ask much of me, and I don't ask much of them."

"Sounds like the perfect arrangement," Jane said with a twitch of her lips.

"I know you think the cats are no replacement for a husband, but they *are* good company."

"That's what I need right now—companionship. Maybe I'll have to consider cats, then.

"Yes you should, seriously!"

Jane touched her stomach. "I think this one is going to keep me so busy that I won't have time to think about cats or husbands." When Gracie smiled back at her, Jane said, "Tell me about Zac's wife. What was she like?" Jane wasn't sure why she wanted to know what Ralene was like; whether it was because she was the woman her husband left her for, or because she wanted to find out what type of woman Zac liked.

"I would describe her as someone who was never settled. She was about to leave the community before they got married. Wait a minute. That's right, she did leave for six months and then came back, got baptized, and said she'd marry him."

"From what I've read if an Amish person leaves after they're baptized they are shunned if they return?"

"That's right. No one is permitted to talk to them and they have to keep separate. They can't even eat with their own families—at the same table. It may seem harsh, but it's only for the best for the person who's being shunned."

Jane couldn't work that out; it seemed harsh to her. "But his wife left before she was baptized, so there was no punishment and no shunning?"

"That's right, in her case. You see it's better for the baptized person to be not spoken to and kept separate so they see the error of their ways. Better to be uncomfortable for a few weeks than not to make it into God's kingdom."

Jane nodded trying to see how the Amish saw things. "It seems complicated."

"It's not; it's really not complicated at all."

"Can you tell me what her personality was like?"

"It was as though she could never settle. After Gia was born she rejected her and didn't want anything to do with her."

Jane gasped, not being able to believe that anyone could reject their own child. "Did she have postnatal depression? I've heard of that happening."

"She refused to see a doctor. I encouraged her to go; I knew something wasn't right."

"I feel sorry for her even though she was the one who stole my husband. But I guess, if it wasn't her, it would've been somebody else."

"If you're interested in our ways, why don't you come to the meeting tomorrow?"

"Yes, I think I might. Zac and Lizzie both said I could go with them if I wanted."

"Good. I hope you go. It'll give you a better understanding of things."

"What should I wear?"

"Probably don't wear jeans."

Jane laughed. "I'd hardly fit into jeans."

"Pants, then. Don't wear pants. Just a dress would be okay, but nothing too revealing."

Jane gave a laugh. "Anything revealing I've got is at home, and I wouldn't be able to fit into those clothes now, anyway."

"Just wear anything. It'll be fine. Just be yourself. We're all people just like you."

"If they're like you and the Yoder family they'll be the friendliest people I've ever met."

Gracie smiled at her.

"I'm nervous about going there. Will anyone try to talk me into joining?"

Gracie shook her head. "We don't go out looking for people to join us. It's not like that. No one's going to talk you into anything. You can just sit back, watch and listen to what goes on."

CHAPTER 12

*One thing have I desired of the Lord,
that will I seek after; that I may dwell in the house of the Lord
all the days of my life, to behold the beauty of the Lord, and to
enquire in his temple.*
Psalm 27:4

THEY TRAVELED to the Sunday meeting in the largest buggy that the Yoders owned. The buggy had room enough for herself, Zac, his parents, and Gia.

"You sit in the front," Lizzie said to Jane.

"I don't mind sitting in the back," Jane said.

"No; you're sitting in the front. I'll help you up." Before Mrs. Yoder could help her into the buggy, Zac was already lifting her up with a hand under her elbow.

. . .

She sat in the buggy and watched Zac finish adjusting the leather straps of the harness. When he finished, he climbed into the front seat beside her. Zac looked at her and smiled before he looked over the back at his parents and daughter.

"Are we ready?" he asked.

"Yes hurry; we don't want to be late," Lizzie said.

"We're never late," Tobias said. "Your mother thinks if we aren't ten minutes early we're late."

Gia giggled, finding what her grandfather said particularly funny.

Jane didn't know whether she should laugh or not, but she couldn't keep the smile from her face. Jane's mother had been very much the same and that habit had helped make Jane punctual as well. There was nothing worse in a client's eyes than their advertising-campaign manager turning up late for an appointment.

As the buggy turned onto the road at the end of the driveway, Jane asked, "How long is the ride?"

"Around twenty minutes," Zac answered.

Lizzie leaned forward. "Just sit back and relax, Jane."

"Yes, I will, I'll do that."

Jane had already heard from the conversation at the breakfast table that the meeting was at Blake Esh's house. There was no church building, as they held the meetings in the homes of various members of the community every second Sunday.

"As you can see, there's no one working in the fields even though it's harvest time."

Jane looked out at the passing fields. "Does that make it harder for you to find people to help you with the building work?"

"Not really. Most of the people coming to help me work as builders, they aren't farmers."

Jane nodded.

Tobias said, "It's hard work bringing in the harvest. I'm glad I don't have to do that anymore."

Jane twisted a little to see Tobias behind her. "You had to work the farm?"

"Yes, when I was a boy. We all had to help no matter what our age. There was always a job for each of us."

As Tobias talked more about harvest, the buggy turned along a dirt driveway and Zac slowed the horse to a walk.

Zac positioned the buggy skilfully alongside the last in a row of buggies.

While Gia's grandparents were busily getting her out of the buggy, Zac leaned over and said, "If you want to leave at any time I'll take you home. Don't feel you need to stay for the whole thing."

"Oh, that's very kind of you. I think I should be okay."

He smiled and said, "It's no trouble; just let me know."

Zac's offer of an escape calmed her nerves a little.

After Jane got out of the buggy, Lizzie was right by her side.

"Just stick with me and you'll be fine," Lizzie said. "Us women sit on one side of the room and the men sit on the other. There's no intermingling."

"That's good to know."

On the walk to the house, Gia took her grandmother's hand and Jane walked on the other side, with Lizzie in the center of the threesome. Lizzie stopped and talked to a couple of people and introduced Jane. Jane glanced back to see that Zac and his father were still at the buggy.

When Lizzie was done talking, she said, "Don't mind Zac and Tobias, they're fiddlers; they're probably tying the horse up just so." Lizzie motioned for Jane to walk into the house.

"You first," Jane said with a little headshake.

Lizzie smiled and walked through the door still holding Gia's hand. They took a seat in the third row from the back.

"Can I sit next to you, Ms. Walker?"

"That's fine with me; is that okay, Lizzie?"

Lizzie nodded. Gia moved passed her grandmother and sat on the other side of Jane. Jane wondered if the meetings weren't terribly boring for a child of Gia's age.

"That's our bishop, the one with the dark beard, and the man next to him is one of our deacons."

After Lizzie had pointed out a few other people, Jane did her best to memorize all the names.

A tall man stood and sang a hymn in a language that Jane recognized as German. For the next song, everyone joined in, after which one of the ministers stood and said a prayer. The bishop made a few announcements and then delivered his sermon.

Jane found it hard to concentrate and harder still to sit on the hard wooden bench with no back. It wasn't easy for a pregnant woman to sit like that. Just as she was contemplating how to let Zac know she was ready to go home, the bishop sat and another man stood and said a prayer—Jane hoped it was a closing prayer.

"It's finished now," Lizzie whispered to her.

Jane nodded and looked down at Gia who'd been quiet the whole time.

"It's over?" Gia asked.

"Yes," Jane said.

Lizzie accompanied Jane outside. "The ladies are preparing food and once the men clear out all the benches, we go back into the house to eat."

"I'm ready for a snack about now." Jane looked around for Zac, wondering if she might catch sight of the women who were interested in him. Once they got back into the house, Jane noticed Zac talking to a woman. She looked around for Gracie, hoping she might let her know if she was one of those women she'd been talking about.

After they'd gotten their food and sat down to eat it, Lizzie told her, "We have easy food on Sundays. We Amish don't work on the Lord's day, but of course, we have to provide for the people who are staying at the B&B."

"It seems a good idea to have the meeting so early in the day because then you have the rest of the day free. What do you normally do on a Sunday afternoon?"

"Tobias and I go visiting."

"Are you two ready?" Zac asked walking up to them.

"I'm ready," Jane said.

"I think we're all set to go," Lizzie said.

Gia took hold of her father's hand.

Once they were in the buggy, Tobias asked, "What did you think of our meeting, Jane?"

"It was a little hard to understand what the bishop was saying and I didn't know what the songs were about because I don't understand any German. Although, I did learn some at school, but that was a long time ago. Everyone was very friendly and so nice."

"You're welcome to come again if you'd like to," Lizzie said.

"I think I'd like that." She felt Zac look at her and she turned and caught his eye. He seemed pleased.

CHAPTER 13

The Lord is my light and my salvation; whom shall I fear?
the Lord is the strength of my life; of whom shall I be afraid?
Psalm 27:1

BACK AT THE HOUSE, after an easy Sunday lunch of salad and cold cuts, Mr. and Mrs. Yoder took Gia with them and went visiting. Jane was convinced that a favorite pastime of the Amish was eating since she'd had three meals before one in the afternoon.

Being Sunday and having no workers present, she and Zac were alone in the large house. The only problem was, Jane didn't know where Zac was. He could've been outside somewhere or in his room and she desperately wanted to talk to him and spend time with him again.

Maybe what she needed was to go back to work. All this free time had led her obsessive-compulsive brain to focus on Zac. And what if he didn't share the feelings that she was developing for him?

She forced all thoughts and images of Zac out of her head and went outside into the garden, determined to get more of her book read.

Jane pulled a white chair around so her back would warm in the sun and the glare wouldn't prevent her from seeing the words on the page. When she had positioned the chair at the optimal angle, she sat, only to see that she was in direct view of Zac and his horse. "Perfect," she grumbled to herself. This isn't going to help me forget him."

He looked over from training his horse and waved, and she gave a smile and a wave back.

Perhaps this could be like a holiday romance—like the romances people had on cruise ships. They could be like two ships that passed in the night. Would that be wrong? Telling herself that she deserved some male attention, she ignored the fact that she was heavily pregnant, pushed herself up, tossed her book on the chair and ambled over to him.

On seeing her approaching, he stopped his horse. "I hope I wasn't bothering you?" he said.

"In what way?"

"Was I too loud giving him commands?"

Jane gave a little laugh. "I didn't hear you at all."

"How's that book coming along? Have you finished it yet?"

She shook her head. "There are too many distractions."

Now it was his turn to laugh. "It's Sunday afternoon and you've got the place to yourself. Well, nearly to yourself, apart from me."

"Maybe I'm not in the mood to read. Mind if I watch you train the horse?"

"You could've watched, but we've done enough for one day." He patted the horse on his neck. "This is Jack."

"Hello, Jack."

"He doesn't talk much."

Jane laughed, and then Zac joined in with her laughter.

"Your cheeks are getting red the more you laugh," he said.

She touched her fingertips to her cheeks, and then pointed at him. "Well, your chin's getting red." She laughed some more at the look on his face.

"Well, so's yours!"

She laughed along with him so much that she had to wipe away a tear. "I haven't laughed so much in years."

It was a silly moment, and she wasn't sure why they both found each other so funny, but it felt good to find something humorous. Her life had become anything but carefree.

When their laughing stopped, she nodded toward the horse. "Can I pat him?"

Zac walked him closer. Jane put her hand out and the horse shied away.

"No. He doesn't like his face patted. Pat him here." He patted him on the side of his neck.

"Bring him a little closer. I can't lean too far over." The fence was right up against Jane's stomach. Once the horse was closer, Jane patted him. "I used to be scared of horses when I was younger. I think it was because they were so big."

"You grew up with them?"

She shook her head. "I've always been a city girl, but my mother was a good horseback rider. She wanted me to be able to ride as well, but it never worked out that way. I wouldn't go near the horses on the two occasions she tried to make me take lessons. After that, she gave up and tried to have me take piano lessons."

"What did you spend your time doing when you were younger?"

Jane was silent while she thought for a while. "My mother was determined to make me good at something. After the piano lessons were a total and complete disaster, she took me ice-skating, and after that, tap dancing classes. Nothing worked out. Then when I was about eleven, my mother gave up. I do like to read, though, and I was one of those weird kids who liked school. What about you? What did you do when you were younger—for fun, or entertainment?"

"I told you I grew up with older brothers. We'd run home from school in the summer and then we'd play until we'd be called in for the evening meal. We'd ride the horses, fish in the river, and play cricket. Then in the colder weather, we'd think up games to play in the barn. Don't get me wrong; it wasn't all play. There were plenty of chores."

"What kind of games?"

He laughed and put his hand to his chin. "We'd jump off the rafters into a pile of hay. I don't know why we liked to do it; I guess it was just fun. And probably because our parents had told us not to do it."

"So you were a rebel?"

"Just a little. The older boys should've been keeping a better watch on me."

"So it was their fault."

"Absolutely."

"Your childhood sounds like it was enjoyable."

"It was and I had hoped that Gia would be the oldest of many children."

"Could you marry again or does your religion forbid that?"

He smiled. "I would like to marry again if God wills it. How about yourself?"

"Would I marry again?"

He nodded.

She leaned forward and patted the horse again. "I found out that there's something more important to me than love."

He tipped his head to one side. "What's that?"

"Trust. Trust is more important because if there's no trust, there's no point to love."

"There's always a point to love."

"No, there isn't. Not for me. Oh, you mean like love your neighbor and all that?"

He nodded.

"For me to marry again, I'd have to fully trust the person."

"I do know what you mean, but life doesn't come with a full warranty. Sometimes we have to trust that things will work out."

Jane kept silent. He was speaking like a man who'd not been hurt or disappointed and Jane knew from talking him before, and with Gracie that Zac had experienced both. How could he seem so unaffected by such things?

"Care to come for a walk with me? I'm just going to turn Jack out into the far paddock."

"Okay."

Zac walked Jack through the gate and waved Jane over. When she'd caught up to him, he started walking.

"Have you heard from your work at all?"

"I haven't. I'm starting to feel like all of that's not so important now."

Zac studied her. "Now that you've been away for a week or so?"

"Yes. I feel like work is a million miles away. I was raised going to church. It was very different from your meetings, but being here has made me start looking at things differently."

He looked over at her once more but said nothing. She wondered what was going through his mind—what did he think about her? Maybe he was thinking he didn't have the luxury of getting away from the community. "Do you ever go away? Visit another community maybe?"

He nodded. "I do every now and again, but I've too many commitments here to do that very often."

"When do those men come to help you?"

"I've got another week on my own and then the others come. Do you think you'll make any permanent changes in your life from your stay here?"

"I hope so. I'm going to make some steps to improve my life. My conversations with Gracie have helped me; she's made me see it's pointless to worry about things that might never happen."

He opened the gate and stepped through with the horse. "Don't come through. I'm coming back out as soon as I take his halter off."

Zac unbuckled the halter and slipped it off the horse's head, then came back through the gate. The horse looked at them both before he turned and walked toward the other horses that were further away in the paddock.

"I like the way everyone in your community cares for one another—and it's genuine, from the heart."

"I don't know any other way; it's just the way I was

raised. I've heard people say that about our community before. We've all grown up together. I guess that's what it is."

CHAPTER 14

*And out of the ground made the Lord God
to grow every tree that is pleasant to the sight, and good for
food; the tree of life also in the midst of the garden,
and the tree of knowledge of good and evil.*
Genesis 2:9

DAYS WENT BY, and the Monday of the following week, Lizzie was called away again to help look after her sick friend.

Tobias looked across the breakfast table at Jane. "What have you got planned for today? More reading?"

"Jane, I had hoped you might like to come with me today to choose some furniture for our B&B," Zac said before Jane answered Tobias.

"I'd love to." She looked at Tobias and said, "I guess

that's what I'm doing. I've finished my first book and now I'm onto a second."

"Your mother is trusting you with choosing the furniture?" Tobias looked at his son in shock.

"She trusts my judgment. Why, don't you?"

Tobias chuckled. "I do, but I didn't know your mother did."

"She said it must be ordered today. Time's marching on. If it isn't ordered today, it won't be ready in time."

"I'm not arguing," Tobias said as he picked up his coffee mug.

"I do have a list of exactly what she wants and what style."

Tobias chuckled. "*That* sounds more like your mother."

"She's trusting me to place the order,"

Tobias nodded.

"Where will we be going to place the order?"

"It's a little over an hour away at my cousin's furniture factory. He's got a team of men working for him now."

"It'll all be Amish made furniture?"

"That's what people expect when they come here, I guess."

"They do," Tobias said.

Gia quietly ate her breakfast looking at each person as they spoke.

"Here, you can hold the list." Zac handed Jane two sheets of paper from his pocket before he climbed into the buggy.

"I usually sit in the front," Gia said. "When there's no one else in the buggy."

"Thank you for giving up your seat, Gia. It was very kind of you."

Jane turned her head as far as she could toward the back seat and caught a glimpse of Gia's smiling face.

As Zac turned the buggy to face down the driveway, Jane looked at the list in her hands. "How do you read your mother's writing?"

"It's hard sometimes, but I can usually work it out." He turned around and said to Gia, "See? That's why you have to go to school; to learn how to write well."

"Didn't *Mammi* go to school?"

"She did, but it seems she didn't practice her writing."

"Let me see, please," Gia said to Jane.

Jane passed the pages over to Gia.

"That is really bad. I can do better than that already."

"Well, you better not tell your grandmother that."

"I won't," Gia said. "I don't want her to get sad."

"She might get very sad if she knows that you can write better than she can, and you're a young girl," Zac said.

Gia giggled.

Jane hoped if she had a daughter she would be as cute and sweet as Gia.

The school was a ten-minute buggy ride up the road. When they pulled up to the schoolhouse, three young young girls ran up to the buggy and waited for Gia to get out.

"I don't want to go to *schul* today, *Dat*."

"You must go."

"Nee." Gia burst into tears.

When another buggy stopped nearby, the three girls turned and ran over to it.

"Do you want me to walk you in, Gia?"

Gia nodded, trying to stop crying.

"Is that okay?" Jane asked Zac who nodded. "I should have asked you first, sorry."

Gia held Jane's hand and Jane got down to her level and said, "What's upsetting you?"

"They say that I talk funny."

"Who says that?"

"Some of the children. My missing tooth makes me talk funny."

Jane realized that the other children must've laughed at the slight lisp Gia had when she spoke. "Gia, don't be upset. They aren't laughing at you or what you're saying. They just think it's strange to hear you talk like that because you didn't sound like that before your tooth fell out."

Gia nodded. "It makes me sad and I don't want them to laugh at me."

Jane licked her lips wondering how she could help. One thing she knew was that she'd have to stand up. Leaning down was hurting too much. "Shall I talk to your teacher?"

Gia nodded again.

"She might not be able to stop some people from laughing, but just remember that one day their baby teeth will fall out and they might sound different too."

Gia giggled. "That would be funny, but I won't laugh at them."

"Come on. Come with me and take me to your teacher."

Once Jane had talked to the teacher, she joined Zac in the buggy.

"Everything sorted out?" he asked.

"She was upset because the children were laughing at her for talking funny."

"Since her tooth fell out?"

Jane nodded. "Yes."

"I should've realized. I wonder why she didn't tell me."

"Sometimes it's easier to talk to a stranger." She smiled at Zac and he smiled back.

CHAPTER 15

Jesus said unto her, I am the resurrection, and the life:
he that believeth in me, though he were dead, yet shall he
live:And whosoever liveth and believeth in me shall never die.
Believest thou this?
John 11:25-26

ON THEIR WAY to the furniture factory, Jane gathered some facts about the B&B so she could help with the marketing and advertising as she'd said she would. "How many bedrooms are there for guests at the B&B?"

"We have eight separate rooms for guests and there are two pairs of two bedrooms that connect to each other."

"So, twelve bedrooms in all?"

"Yes and there is room for expansion with the cabin idea that I've had."

"That sounds like a good idea, and you've certainly got room for it."

"It keeps me busy, thinking about new options," he said.

"Thanks for inviting me today. It's nice to see some more places before I go home."

"What do you think of the place so far—the whole county?"

"It's peaceful and quiet here; nothing like what I'm used to." Jane laughed. It took me quite a while to get used to not worrying about work, but I haven't thought about the O'Connor account or Derek for days."

"Is he the one you're worried about stealing your job from you?"

"Yes. Derek. I haven't thought about him and how he's trying to get rid of me, either."

"That's good."

"I suppose it is." There seemed a rhythm to the Amish way of life, much like the clip-clopping of the horse's hooves—which was a lovely way to travel. Even though it wasn't fast, it didn't bother anyone because everything here had its own rhythm, and things happened when they happened.

After a moment of silence Zac said, "Jane, I've been thinking about your work situation."

She laughed. "And I'm trying to forget it."

"I've been thinking you should tell your boss that

you suspect that Derek suggested you come here so you'd be reminded of your husband. Coming to a place where you'd be reminded of your husband being unfaithful was not going to give you the rest your boss wanted you to have."

"I know, you're right, but I've been in situations like this before with men like Derek. Derek will insist it was a coincidence and he'll make me look like a crazy woman. Unfortunately, he's a convincing liar."

"Even if your boss thinks you're accusing Derek wrongly, deep down, he'll have a question mark in his mind in regard to Derek. If he does something else like this again, your boss will realize what you said was right." He glanced over at her and she saw the sincerity in his eyes. He continued, "I've never found that keeping quiet about something helps any situation.

"I hear what you're saying, but you've never been in the corporate world." His life was much simpler and he'd have no idea of the complexities that existed in her world. A woman at the top of her game in a men's world was a target for people like Derek.

"Human nature is always the same. The darkness in the world comes from the sinful nature of man."

"The difference is that people like you probably fight against such a thing, but Derek doesn't. He wouldn't feel guilt or remorse, and he wouldn't care about playing fair. Thanks for your suggestion, though; I'll keep it in mind." No, she wouldn't. Zac had no idea the levels people like Derek would go to, but she couldn't tell Zac so without offending him.

He chuckled.

She looked over at him. "What?"

"You're not going to listen to me or take any of my advice."

Jane raised her eyebrows. Was she that transparent? "I will think about it."

"If you're reading the situation with Derek correctly, I don't see that you've got anything to lose by stating your suspicions to your boss. If he respects you, he'll listen to you and consider what you have to say."

"And if he doesn't listen and puts it down to paranoia and pregnancy hormones?"

He took his eyes off the road for a moment. "Do you really want to work for someone like that?"

A shiver ran down Jane's spine. "Tyrone's a friend as well as my boss."

"A friend? There's even more reason for you to tell him what you suspect, and for him to listen to you."

Work was work, and she'd been employed by some ruthless people in the past. There was never any question about morals or scruples in the workplace. Sure, everyone acted like they were playing fair as they crawled their way to the top; it was a juggling act of keeping one eye on your back and the other on the top job.

"In a perfect world, you'd be right."

"Nothing is ever perfect. I think it's up to us to

choose what we're willing to put up with in life. Do you want someone like Derek in your life?"

"No, I don't. Of course, I don't."

"If you continue the way you're going then you're going to have to put up with people like him."

"I see what you're saying. Tell my boss about him and it's either he goes or I go?"

He laughed. "That puts your friend in an awkward position. Tell him what you think is going on. If this man, Tyrone, is really your friend, he'll respect you for your honesty." He looked over to his right. "Ah, here we are."

As he guided the horse and buggy into the large parking lot of the furniture factory, she said, "You've given me a lot to think about."

He stopped his buggy, looked over at her with his smiling brown eyes. "It was just a suggestion. You do what you feel is right. Now, let's go and choose this furniture. If I get anything wrong, I'll tell my mother it was your fault."

Jane laughed. "Now that's the kind of behavior I'm used to."

As soon as they were in the door, an Amish man approached them. He was similar in build to Zac, but much older. As soon as they shook hands, Zac introduced Micah to Jane.

"Jane is here to help me choose this furniture. She's

a guest at the B&B."

"Good!" Micah's eyes dropped to the list that was still in Jane's hands. "Is this the list?"

"Yes," Zac said. "This is what we need, and Mamm's leaving it to me to pick the wood. She said nothing too dark, but the final choice will be mine."

Micah looked at Jane. "And you will have the final choice after Zac's final choice?"

Zac laughed. "Jane's kindly offered to help me choose everything."

"We both know women have the final say, Zac."

"That's true."

Micah read from the list that Jane handed to him, "Eight pairs of single beds..." He looked up. "What happened to the other furniture you had?"

"*Mamm* sold it. She wants a fresh look, and to have all the rooms furnished the same."

Micah raised his eyebrows. "Okay. So you're going to choose the styles and the wood?"

Zac nodded.

"That's a lot of pressure. Where's Lizzie?"

"She's at Deirdre's house—she's sick again."

"That's no good."

Zac said, "You're both going to have to help me. If I get it wrong, I'll hear about it for years."

"I'll show you what's been the most popular. You can't go too far wrong. Follow me; we'll start with the bedroom furniture." Micah headed off to the far end of the warehouse showroom.

CHAPTER 16

And fear not them which kill the body, but are not able to kill the soul: but rather fear him which is able to destroy both soul and body in hell.
Matthew 10:28

AN HOUR AND A HALF LATER, they were driving away from the warehouse.

"Thank you for all your help."

"I hope I helped you make the right choices."

"I'm confident we've made the right decisions. Now, you must be hungry."

"I'm always hungry."

"There's a nice place just up a little further where we can have lunch. That is if you like hamburgers and fries—nice ones."

"I do." Jane was pleased that she was going to be spending more time with Zac. She wondered again if he knew she was growing so fond of him.

ONCE THEY WERE SITTING with their hamburger lunches in front of them, Jane hoped he wouldn't mind her asking some questions that had been plaguing her mind.

"Can I ask you something about Ralene?"

He finished the mouthful he was chewing. "Yes. You can ask me anything."

Now that he'd said that, everything left her mind. "There are so many things racing through my mind. I suppose there are many things I want to know that you won't be able to answer. I guess the biggest thing in my mind was that they'd been hiding their affair for a whole year."

"Do you want to know if I had any suspicions?"

Jane nodded. "I was suspicious of Sean all the time, and I even checked on him, but found nothing. I would've thought he was having multiple affairs, but I never would've guessed that he was having an intense affair."

"I know how you feel. You're feeling just as betrayed as I am and wondering where you went wrong —what you could've done differently."

"That's right; I do. He was always telling me I was

in love with my job and not with him. I know I didn't give him enough attention."

"I had no suspicions like you had. Ralene was troubled, I knew that much. She could've slipped away to meet someone every day. She was always leaving Gia with people." He sighed and then wiped his hands on a napkin. "For the first few weeks after she died, I kept going back and seeing all the wrong decisions I made—they played out in front of my eyes. Firstly, that I shouldn't have married her. She was reluctant, but I thought she was the right woman for me—I was very protective of her. I thought she'd grow up and mature once we were married and had children. She didn't change at all."

This was the first time she'd seen Zac upset.

He looked up at her and said, "We both probably did things that didn't help our situations, but we weren't the ones who crossed the line."

"I know that, but that doesn't make it easier. I keep wondering why he chose the other woman, Ralene, and didn't stay with me. It makes me feel that I wasn't good enough." She'd never given voice to her feelings before, but if anyone could understand what she was feeling and going through, it would be Zac.

"Maybe they both chose the unknown which seemed more exciting than what they already had. I think it was an escape for both of them."

She looked down at her food and ripped off a piece of hamburger bun wondering if he'd experienced low self esteem from his spouse leaving him, just as she had. "Sean was escaping from me?"

"From life, from you—who knows? We're never going to have all our questions answered. All we can do in life is learn from any mistakes we've made, and then move past them."

Jane's lips turned slightly upward at the corners. "It's the moving past them that I have a problem with."

"It's going to take time."

Jane nodded. "I'm always after the quick fix—the fast track."

"Maybe it's time to do things differently."

"You're right. I know you're right. How come you're so wise?"

He laughed and picked up his hamburger. "It's logical. I was going to say male logic, but I thought I might get hamburger all over my head."

"You would've."

"If one way of doing something isn't working, it's time to change." He bit into his hamburger. When he finished chewing, he continued, "I might sound like I have all the answers, but I don't. I'm fighting off bitterness in my heart that Ralene could leave Gia and run away without a word to her. All she did was leave me a note that she was leaving with Sean. From what you've told me, your husband at least had the decency to tell you to your face that he was leaving, and leaving you for another woman."

He was right. Jane picked up her soda and sipped

on the straw. She would've felt much worse if Sean hadn't told her he was leaving. But no matter how bad a wife she'd been, she was having his baby. Would that have meant anything to him, had she told him?

SOMETHING CAME into Jane's mind that Gracie had said to her, and she said, "I suppose you think that everything that happens is God's will?"

"Yes, I do."

"I guess that makes you okay with whatever happens?"

"It still hurts when things don't go my way, or someone I love is harmed."

Jane rearranged some of the fillings on her hamburger so she could eat it without it going everywhere.

When they were both finished, Jane said, "It's been nice spending time with you today. Thank you."

"Thank you for coming with me. I enjoy your company—very much."

When they headed back in the buggy, their conversation was devoid of late spouses.

Before Jane got out of the buggy, she said, "I'm glad I came here. Even though I didn't want to leave work, I'm happy I did."

"I'm pleased too."

Zac had brought Jane right to the front door of the

bed and breakfast. "I'll see you at the evening meal," Zac said when she got out of the buggy.

Jane went to her room and looked out the window to see Zac's buggy heading down to the barn area where he would unhitch the horse.

She pushed the easy chair over and sat down intending to see what he was doing. No sooner had she sat down then she saw another buggy coming to the house. It was Lizzie and Tobias. Feeling like some company, Jane left her bedroom and made herself comfortable in the sitting room hoping that Lizzie would come in and speak to her.

Just like Zac had done, Tobias had brought Lizzie right to the front door, going by the sound of the horse's hooves. She heard the front door open and Lizzie's footsteps. Then Lizzie appeared in the doorway of the sitting room.

"How has your day been?" Jane asked.

"Tiring." She walked in and sat opposite Jane in an easy chair. "My friend has her good days and her bad days. Today was one of her better days and I've been trying to help her organize her house to make things easier for her.

Jane didn't like to inquire what was wrong with Lizzie's friend.

"Did you go with Zac?"

"I did."

"That's good. He told me he was going to ask you. I hope you helped him make the right choices."

Jane cringed. "I hope so, too. Both Zac and I liked the suggestions that his cousin made."

"I could've done it tomorrow. I suppose another day wouldn't have made a difference, but one day Zac will be taking over this place so he might as well start taking some of the responsibility."

"I'm glad you have confidence in me to help with the choices."

"It doesn't hurt to have a customer's viewpoint." Lizzie stood up and pressed a button on the wall. "I think it's time for some hot tea and something to eat."

"Sounds good." Jane couldn't eat much in one sitting. She'd found it better to eat a little at a time, and eat more often to avoid heartburn.

When one of the staff appeared, Jane realized that the button must ring a bell in the kitchen. Lizzie ordered tea and food for them, and while they waited for it to arrive, Jane told Lizzie all about the furniture she'd helped Zac order.

CHAPTER 17

*For whether we live, we live unto the Lord;
and whether we die, we die unto the Lord: whether we live
therefore, or die, we are the Lord's.*
Romans 14:8

"I KNOW what you might like, Jane," Lizzie said.

"What's that?"

"I'm helping out a lady on a quilting bee next week because she's not too well. Why don't you come with me?"

"When is it?"

"Tuesday next week."

"Okay. I'd like to see what happens at a quilting bee."

Lizzie giggled. "A lot of quilting, and gossip, and eating."

"Sounds like it might be fun."

"Good! Now, are you still having appointments with Gracie?"

"I haven't booked any more. I must admit I do like the idea of using a midwife. It's a shame she can't travel to New York."

"Why don't you come back here to have the baby? You can stay here as my guest. Of course, you'd have to be here a couple of weeks before your due date just in case of an early arrival. We have a room upstairs that we don't often let out because it's small, but it would be a good place for you to have your baby."

"Really? You wouldn't mind?"

"Mind? I'd love it. You've been like a bright light sent to us. We were all in the doldrums with what had happened to Ralene, on top of dealing with the renovations, and then that friend of yours talked us into having you stay. I'm glad we agreed."

"So am I, in so many ways. Can I let you know? I'll have to give it some serious thought and also have another talk with Gracie."

"The offer's there."

Jane had always thought the Amish would be private people or even secretive, but the Yoders were all open, friendly and honest. Zac had opened his heart to her and talked about things that he might not have told anyone else.

It was after lunch the following day when Jane had the next chance to be alone with Zac. Gia was at school and Zac and she were in the sitting room in front of the fire.

"I miss a fireplace. I don't like the work of cleaning it, though. We had one when I was growing up."

"Do you live in an apartment?"

Jane nodded. "I do—with central heating. Your mother is taking me to a quilting bee next week."

His lips twitched at the corners. "Somehow I can't see you going to one of those."

"Have you been to one?"

He laughed. "Quilting bees are for women who like to talk."

"And sew," Jane added.

"From what I've heard, not much sewing goes on."

"I'll soon find out."

"My mother invited you?"

Jane nodded.

He shook his head. "That surprises me."

"Why?"

"The woman are all plain women and you're…"

She arched an eyebrow.

"You're not very Amish, in fact, you're the opposite."

"I could become Amish, couldn't I—if I chose?"

He chuckled. "You could, and people have joined us from time to time."

"How would I go about joining?"

"You'd have to speak to the bishop. Then he'd suggest you stay with an Amish family for a few months to see if you think you'd be suited to live as we do and abide by the *Ordnung*."

"I've heard about the *Ordnung*. They're a list of unwritten rules, as far as I could ascertain."

"It's our way of living."

"I've got a head start because I've been here for a few weeks already."

He laughed. "Staying at a bed and breakfast is not the same as staying with an Amish family. You'd have to leave everything you know behind."

"I might have nothing to go back to." She lowered her head and glanced at Zac from underneath her dark lashes. He seemed to be interested in her, but she hoped she wasn't reading him incorrectly. She daren't tell him his mother had offered for her to give birth at the B&B.

"How are the men doing?"

"Men?"

"Your workers? I haven't been driven crazy with hammering or dust like you said I would be."

"They've been delayed a few more days because of

the plumbing work. The plumber has given his word he'll be here tomorrow."

"I'll keep out of their way."

"They'll be working at the other end of the house to start with. In the old section, which isn't the old, old section, it's the new old section."

Jane joined in his laughter. "I know what you mean, not the stone part of the house where we are now."

"Exactly."

They both heard a car and turned around. Jane looked harder and saw that the car was Tyrone's black Mercedes.

"It's my boss, Tyrone."

Tyrone pulled the car into the parking lot and Jane hurried to him. "Tyrone," she called out a little too loudly. She looked back at Zac, who had been following close behind. "He's been my boss for awhile."

Once he'd stepped out of the car and caught sight of Jane, he opened his arms widely. She stepped into his arms and he enclosed her in them.

She took a step back from his hug. "What are you doing here?"

"I keep my word. I told you I'd come and visit. Don't you remember?"

"That's right, but I never thought you'd actually... I thought that was just something you were saying."

Tyrone laughed at her. Then he looked over her shoulder at Zac. Jane turned around to see Zac standing right behind her and she introduced the two men. They shook hands, all the while looking warily at one another.

"Is this your B&B?" Tyrone asked Zac.

"My parents own it," he replied. "We've been taking good care of Jane and keeping a close eye on her."

"Thank you, but now that I'm here, I can take over that job."

Jane sensed tension between the two men. "How long are you here for, Tyrone?"

He shot Zac a glare, and then looked back at her. "I can't stay. I'm only here for a few hours."

"You drove all this way just for a few hours?"

"I wanted to see how you were rather than just phoning you." He looked her up and down. "You're looking well, and the baby has grown."

Zac took another step forward. "As I said, we're looking after her."

"I'm sure you are." Tyrone took his eyes off Zac and focused on Jane. "Is there somewhere we can talk in private?"

Jane felt embarrassed over Tyrone's rudeness and Zac's apparent newfound possessiveness. "We could go into the living room. Come with me and I'll see if we can arrange a cup of tea." She looked around at Zac. "Will you join us?"

He shook his head. "I've got work."

"What about a stiff drink instead of a cup of tea?" Tyrone said as he walked to the house with Jane.

Jane laughed. "I'll see what we can arrange. Excuse us, Zac." She looked after Zac as he walked away.

Zac called over his shoulder, "I'll see you later tonight, Jane."

Tyrone put his arm around Jane's shoulders as they walked. Once they were seated in the living room, he said, "I'm here because I want you to come back with me."

"You do?"

He gave a sharp nod. "I think you should come back."

"Right now? What's going on? Why do you want me to come back all of a sudden?"

"It's Derek and the O'Connor account." He rubbed his nose, and from his edgy body language, Jane knew he was lying.

"What's happening with the O'Connor account?" she asked.

"Derek's not handling it at all well. I need you back, Jane, and I need you back now!"

CHAPTER 18

*And God shall wipe away all tears from their eyes;
and there shall be no more death, neither sorrow, nor crying,
neither shall there be any more pain:
for the former things are passed away.*
Revelation 21:4

THIS IS what Jane had wanted—to go back and take over the O'Connor account. But now that she was getting to know Zac and feeling at peace for the first time in a very long time, she wasn't ready to leave. Her reluctance must have shown.

"What's the matter with you? Don't you want to come back? You didn't want to come here. Why are you so reluctant to leave? I thought you'd pack your things and head for the car as soon as I told you I wanted you back at work."

She inhaled deeply. How could she tell him so he'd understand?

"You've been here for weeks already; all I'm asking you to do is come back early. Am I asking too much or do you think that your pregnancy hormones have taken over?"

She shook her head. "Not at all. I'll come back. You don't want me to come back in the car with you right now, do you?"

"That's what I had in mind; unless you want to go back by bus again.

"No, the bus trip was awful."

The housemaid brought in a tray of tea, and a glass of apple cider for Tyrone.

He lifted up the apple cider and held it up to the light. "Is this alcoholic?" he asked the housemaid.

"I'm sorry, I don't know, sir."

He took a sip. "My educated guess is 'no.'"

"Thank you, Mary," Jane said to the young woman.

The young woman smiled at her before she left the room.

"Surely you can do without a drink for one day."

"I can, but I've had a long drive. I deserve to be able to relax with a drink."

"I'd rather you not drink since I'm going back with you." She wanted to avoid anything that might contribute to an accident since her mother and her husband had died in car accidents.

"Yes, of course. I'm sorry. I don't know what I was thinking." He took a mouthful of apple cider. "Not bad, actually." Tyrone looked across at her. "Are you going to pack? We want to get going before dark at least."

She looked at her tea that she hadn't had a chance to drink. "I've got some people I need to say goodbye to."

"Who?"

"Zac and his daughter. Wait, she's at school. Can we wait until after school before we leave? Then there's Gracie, who's become a good friend."

He shook his head. "I don't think anyone can become a friend in such a short space of time."

"You don't know these people. They have no falsity, they have no agendas, they…"

He raised his hand. "Spare me. I tell you what. How about I stay here for the night and we leave first thing in the morning. Will that make you happy?"

She nodded. "That would be better except they don't have any places here for you to stay. I have the only room; everything else is still under renovation."

"I'll find something nearby, and then I'll pick you up at eight in the morning."

"Thank you, Tyrone."

When Tyrone left to find somewhere to stay, Jane went to find Zac to let him know that she was leaving the next day. She found him packing up his tools in the barn.

"Why are you going so soon?" Zac asked.

"Tyrone needs me back at work."

"Is that what you want?"

She shrugged her shoulders. "That's what I wanted a few weeks ago."

"And now?" When she didn't answer, he continued, "Does Tyrone need you back at work, or is it Tyrone himself who can't do without you?"

Jane studied his face as his jaw clenched. "Don't be like that, Zac. There's nothing between Tyrone and…"

"It's not my concern. You don't have to answer any of my questions."

Jane swallowed hard; she wanted it to be his concern and she had to let him know that there was nothing at all between Tyrone and herself. "He wanted me to go with him today, but he's agreed to wait until the morning. That way I can say goodbye to Gracie, Gia, and your parents."

He dropped his hammer and put hands on his hips. "I'm going to really miss you, Jane. Do you think you'll ever come back this way?"

"Do you want me to?"

His face softened into a smile. "I do; very much."

"Then I will come back."

"Can I call you?"

Jane felt her insides light up. "I'll give you the number of my cell phone."

"Good. Care to come with me while I collect Gia from school?"

She nodded. "I'd love to.

"Gia's going to be upset that you're leaving."

"I was always leaving. It's just that I'm going a little bit earlier."

"I guess we all knew that, but lately I haven't wanted to think about it."

She was pleased that he was letting her know that he was fond of her too. "Would it be too much to ask that we stop by Gracie's house so I can say goodbye?"

"We'll do that right after I collect Gia."

"Thank you."

"I'll meet you outside the house in twenty minutes. I've just got a little more work to do."

Jane headed back to the house to tell Lizzie and Tobias that she was leaving early.

∽

AFTER ZAC HAD COLLECTED Gia from school, Gia and Zac waited patiently while Jane knocked on Gracie's door to say goodbye.

"I can't believe you're going."

"Lizzie said I could have the baby there."

"I know, she told me about it. And the offer is still there for me to deliver your baby. If that's what you want."

"I'm going to give it a lot of thought once I get back home."

"When are you going to decide—you haven't got much time left?"

"I know. It won't take me long to decide. I haven't mentioned anything to Zac that I might come back to have the baby at the B&B. I didn't want to say anything to him in case I decided against it."

"I understand completely. Just keep in touch." Gracie handed her a card with her phone number on it. "Here's my phone number. Call me any time you need anything—any advice or an opinion on anything."

Jane took the card from her and then hugged her goodbye.

CHAPTER 19

*Being born again, not of corruptible seed,
but of incorruptible, by the word of God,
which liveth and abideth for ever.*
1 Peter 1:23

BREAKFAST WAS SPENT IN SILENCE. The only one who talked was Gia, who asked Jane if she could stay longer. Both Gia and Jane cried, and Zac didn't look happy either.

Jane didn't linger when the time came to say goodbye. Everyone gave her a hug while Tyrone put her bag in the car and then waited for her. Once she walked to the car, she didn't look back.

Tyrone's car zoomed down the driveway, while Jane cried.

"I've never seen you show this much emotion."

"It was an emotional stay," she said wiping her eyes. "I'll get over it."

Tyrone glanced over at her. "Seems I came just in time."

Jane said nothing.

Half an hour into the drive back, Tyrone said, "Did I sense something was happening between you and that Zac fellow?"

Jane laughed it off. "Of course not. He's Amish!"

Tyrone glanced over at her and she knew that he didn't believe a word of what she said. He knew something was going on between the two of them. "I think you're lonely since Sean died. I didn't know Sean's death would've affected you in that way."

"Of course, it affected me. My husband died, and my child is going to be fatherless."

"I know it affected you; I meant I didn't know it had affected you in that way. That you'd become vulnerable and succumb to the interest of the first man who came along."

"That's a dreadful thing to say."

"I didn't mean it. Sorry I spoke." After twenty minutes of silence, Tyrone spoke again. "You could marry again you know, and you don't have to marry an Amish man."

"That's the last thing on my mind. I can't think of anything like that right now when I'm so close to giving birth."

"You're not *that* close, are you? You've still got a few more weeks work left."

"Yes, and my work won't suffer up until I go on maternity leave. I plan to leave two weeks before my due date."

"Yes, I know."

Even though Jane knew she'd miss Zac and the rest of his family, she was glad to be home in her own apartment with her own belongings.

The next day it was back to work as usual.

Mid-morning of the first day she found she wasn't excited about the work anymore. It didn't mentally stimulate her the way it used to.

Neither did she care that Derek had done an unusually good job on the O'Connor account. In fact, she was pleased because if she left, her clients would be in good hands. If Derek wanted her job, he could have it as far as she was concerned. Maybe it was the pregnancy hormones affecting her, she didn't know, but all that was uppermost on her mind was what it might be like to marry Zac and have a family with him.

"Well, what was it like in the middle of nowhere?"

She looked up to see her personal assistant, Jenny, perch herself on the edge of the desk with two take-out coffee cups. She handed one to Jane. "Decaf."

Jane laughed as she took the decaf. "It wasn't exactly in the middle of nowhere. It was nice and calm and I miss it and the people."

"Really?" Jenny pulled a face.

"Yes really."

"Do you want to hear the gossip?"

" Gossip about what?"

"Derek and what he's been doing while you've been away."

"Yes tell me what he's been up to."

Jenny proceeded to tell her all about Derek and what else had happened since she'd been gone.

Jane left work that day wishing she hadn't left the B&B so early. If she had stayed, maybe she could have developed some kind of a relationship with Zac—a relationship beyond friendship.

When she got home she decided that she would have her baby at the B&B. She took her diary out of her bag and flipped through the pages until she found the marked date—two weeks before her due date. Tomorrow she would call Lizzie and tell her that she would happily accept her kind offer of having the baby at the B&B, and to expect her on that day. Then her next call would be to Gracie accepting her offer. Jane would ask them both to keep it quiet.

When her cell phone rang, she looked down at the caller ID. It said 'Zac,' but maybe it was someone else from the B&B.

"Hello?"

"Hello, Jane. It's Zac."

"Zac! It's nice to hear from you." Her heart pumped against her chest at hearing his voice.

"How's New York?"

"It's busy and stressful—just the same as when I left."

He chuckled. "You should move here. Raise your child in the fresh air with good food."

Jane laughed. *Ask me to marry you and I will*, she mentally projected down the phone. "Maybe I will someday. I'll surprise you."

"I hope you don't mind me calling you."

"Of course not; that's why I gave you my phone number. Call me any time." Right at that moment, the phone disconnected. She looked down at her phone to see the battery had gone dead. She said a rude word before she stood up and plugged the phone into the charger.

A few minutes later, the phone came to life, but there was no missed call from Zac. She hoped that he didn't think she'd hung up on him.

The next morning, the first thing she did was to check her phone. There were no missed calls from Zac, but there was a voice message. She listened to the message and it was from Zac saying that they'd been accidentally disconnected and he'd call again another time. That was all he said. She listened to the message another three times to hear his voice.

That day, Jane did something she'd never done in her life—she called in sick. She couldn't face going to work—Jane didn't want to see Derek or have to worry about what he'd done or not done in her absence.

The lawyer phoned and said he hadn't been able to

trace what had become of the money Sean had received from cashing in his insurance policy. Jane instructed him to stop searching for it. It was a waste of his time and her money. All Jane cared about now was going back and being close to Zac.

CHAPTER 20

*Surely goodness and mercy shall follow
me all the days of my life:
and I will dwell in the house of the Lord for ever.*
Psalm 23:6

THE WEEKS LEADING up to the birth had been torturous for Jane. She'd gone from being a workaholic to hating her work—not able to prevent herself from thinking about Zac. The bright spots in her world were the phone calls from Zac each night. He would talk about life and God, anything at all, and she'd listen. One of their conversations had lasted two hours. He'd told her more about God, the community and the ways of the Amish. In their last conversation, he'd asked her if she ever thought she might be able to live in the community.

Now she was on her way back down to Lancaster County and the Yoders' B&B for the birth of the baby. Just as Gracie had suggested, she'd had fortnightly visits with the doctor to monitor her baby's health. All was fine with her and the baby.

Zac still had no idea she was on her way back by bus. She hoped it would be a nice surprise. Tyrone had offered to drive, but to avoid an uncomfortable scene between Tyrone and Zac; she'd opted to go by bus.

Tyrone was suspicious that there was something going on between Zac and herself, which there wasn't—at least not officially, but Jane had wished there were.

Thinking about seeing Zac again prevented Jane from getting any sleep on the bus.

When the taxi took her from the bus station to the B&B, Lizzie was waiting at the front door.

"Oh, you have gotten a lot bigger." Lizzie giggled. "We've got everything ready for you. You can stay in your old room and when the time comes for the baby, we've got that room ready for you."

Jane put her arms around Lizzie and gave her a hug. "Thank you for everything. It's so good to see you again."

"I haven't told Zac you're coming; is that what you wanted?"

"Yes, that's exactly what I wanted. I didn't want him to know."

Tobias walked out into the reception area and seemed surprised to see her. "Jane?"

"Yes, it's me."

"I had no idea you were coming."

"Here I am."

"She's having her baby right here at the B&B," Lizzie said to Tobias, who was clearly hearing it for the first time.

Tobias looked delighted. "That's wonderful. I'm so glad you've come back to visit us. Does Gracie know?"

Jane gave a little giggle.

"Who do you think is going to deliver the baby? Not me!" Lizzie said to Tobias.

"Yes it's all been arranged," Jane said.

Tobias left them alone.

Jane asked, "Where is Zac?"

"Zac's left us for a while."

"What do you mean? He's gone?"

"He's coming back. He's visiting someone."

"Who?" Jane had deliberately not taken his calls for the past two weeks because she thought she might give the surprise away that she was coming there to give birth. Now she knew she'd made a bad decision. He obviously thought that she was no longer interested in him. Maybe he'd gone to another community to look for a wife.

Jane put a hand over her heart.

"What is it, Jane?"

"I just feel a little cold."

"Come and warm yourself by the fire. I'll get a nice cup of hot tea for both of us. How does that sound?"

Jane nodded. Once they were in the living room, Jane asked. "Can I use my cell phone in here?"

"Of course, you can."

"Good! I'll just call Gracie and let her know I'm here."

Lizzie rang the bell letting the girls know that she wanted something from the kitchen.

Gracie wasn't home, so Jane left a message on her answering machine. "Hi Gracie, it's Jane I'm at the B&B. Come and see me when you can." She ended the call.

When Jane was sitting down with Lizzie, having a cup of tea, Jane asked Lizzie questions about the B&B and heard all about the renovations.

"I'm so sorry I wasn't here to help you with that opening night you had planned. I really wanted to help, but my boss arrived unexpectedly." Jane felt bad that she'd only just now remembered her offer to help—back then she'd left without a word or apology for not being able to help.

"Don't concern yourself about that."

"So you've got no idea where Zac went?"

"No! He's a grown man; he doesn't tell me everything."

"Did Gia go with him?"

"No, she's here with us. He said it would only be a couple of days, and he left yesterday."

Gracie put a hand over her stomach when she felt a pain.

"Is it time? You're not having the baby now, are you?"

She shook her head. "I've been having slight pains for the last few days. Gracie said it's quite normal to have contractions—that aren't really birthing contractions when the time is close. They're practice contractions apparently."

"Are you sure that's all they are?"

"I hope so. Otherwise, I'd be in more pain. Wouldn't I?"

"You should get Gracie to check you over."

"I've left a message on her machine. I'm sure she'll be over soon as she gets the message."

~

GRACIE CAME LATER THAT DAY, as soon as she'd gotten the message. To Jane's surprise, Gracie told her she was in labor.

"I can't be." Jane pushed herself up from the bed and looked from Gracie to Lizzie, who was still in the room. "I'm not in any real pain."

"Not yet," Lizzie said, eyeing her sympathetically.

Jane didn't like the sound of that. "So I'm having my baby now? How far away?"

"How long is a piece of string?" Gracie answered.

"This time tomorrow, you should be sitting here with your baby in your arms. Or, maybe in a few hours."

Jane felt both fear and excitement. Fear of the unknown outweighed her excitement. She hoped she'd made the right decision to have the baby away from the hospital.

Lizzie stepped forward and touched her on her shoulder. "It might be a bit to go through, but you'll have your baby at the end of it."

The baby she'd never intended to have—the baby who had been a pure surprise and the one thing in her life that she hadn't planned for.

～

LIZZIE HAD OFFERED to stay with Jane throughout the birth and Jane was glad to have her there. It was five hours after the midwife had gotten there that Jane's contractions had intensified. Jane no longer had her mind on Zac and where he was. All she could think about was the pains that were wracking her body and wondering when it would all end.

"This part's the worst," Lizzie whispered to her as she mopped Jane's forehead with a washcloth. "When you get to push you'll feel better."

Jane looked at her and nodded.

"Walk around Jane, and things might move quicker."

"Will it be more painful?"

"It'll be over quicker."

Jane didn't know which was worse, but opted for the 'being over quicker.' She walked around the room stopping as her body was gripped by contractions.

"You can walk through them," Gracie said.

No, I can't, Jane thought, not being able to talk. It was twenty minutes later that Jane had the urge to push.

"Wait while I examine you."

"I can't!" Jane screamed as the urge to bear down was greater than anything she could've imagined.

"I can see the baby's head," Gracie said after Jane had stopped pushing. "You can push on the next contraction."

Jane was too tired to tell her that she'd had no intention of trying not to push. Her body was forcing her to push.

Twenty more minutes went by and then, with one last push, Jane's baby boy was taking his first breath.

"He's a boy!" Lizzie squealed and with that, the baby howled. "He's got good lungs too."

Gracie wrapped the baby in a cloth and placed him against Jane's chest.

"Is he okay?" That was all Jane wanted to know. "Is he healthy?"

"He's healthy and well."

"And he's beautiful and so tiny," Lizzie said. " I forgot how tiny they are."

Jane looked down at her baby and wrapped her arms

around him. He had a wrinkled face, and his bright eyes were looking into hers. "He's looking at me."

"They can't see anything for days," Lizzie said peering over Jane's shoulder at the baby.

"He's looking right at me! Hello, my little son. I'm your Mom." A tear trickled down Jane's face, all the pain and all the bad things she'd ever gone through meaning nothing now. The baby in her arms was all that mattered. After Jane had cuddled him for a while, Gracie took him, cut his cord and cleaned him up. When he was all cleaned up, with diaper and clothes on, Gracie covered him in a wrap and handed him back to Jane.

"Will I feed him now?"

"If you'd like to. There's no rush. I'll clean up this room. You might as well stay in this one tonight. He's a beautiful baby, Jane."

"He is." Jane couldn't take her eyes off him. "Thank you for staying with me through everything, Lizzie. You've been so kind to me."

Lizzie patted her on the shoulder. "Does the baby have a name yet?"

"I've always liked the name Matthew."

"Matthew's a good name," Lizzie said, and Gracie agreed.

That night, after Jane had fed Matthew and he was sleeping, her thoughts turned to Zac. Where was he? She got into bed and stared at Matthew beside her in his crib.

It would've been nice for Matthew to have a father and for her to have a husband.

EARLY THE NEXT MORNING, Lizzie opened Jane's door slightly and peeped into her room. "You're awake?"

"Yes. I've been awake most of the night. I think Matthew doesn't know that night time is for sleeping."

"I'll watch him after breakfast, and then you can get some sleep."

"Would you? That would be marvelous."

"You have a visitor."

"Is it Gia?"

"No. Gia is staying at her uncle's house. I thought it best she not be around while you were giving birth."

Jane nodded and Lizzie stepped aside to let Zac poke his head in the door.

"It's me," he said.

She couldn't keep the smile from her face. "Come in."

He walked through the doorway and closed the door behind him. "Are you okay?"

She swallowed hard and nodded. Then the baby in the crib took his attention. "He's lovely and so, so tiny."

"I've called him Matthew."

He smiled and then kneeled beside her. "I had no

idea you were having the baby here. I went to New York to find you."

"You did?"

"You weren't taking my calls and I didn't know what to think. I phoned your work and spoke to Tyrone, who said he hadn't seen you in a while."

"That's not true!"

"I figured as much, but I didn't know what was true. The only thing I could do was come to you. Then I couldn't find you."

"I'm sorry to put you to so much trouble."

"It's no trouble. Don't you know what you mean to me?"

Her heart pumped wildly.

"I went to New York to ask you a question."

Please say you want to marry me. "What question?"

He looked into her eyes and took her hand. "These past two weeks of not knowing where you were, or how you were, it's been just torturous. I can't go through that again, Jane. I want to look after you, you and Matthew. I want us and our children to be a family, and be happy."

"Really?"

He smiled. "Jane, will you marry me?" He shut his eyes tightly and then opened them. "Just say 'yes.'"

Peace flooded her entire being. Matthew would have a father and she would have a husband—one she could trust with her heart and her life. Zac was her answer to prayer. "I will. Yes, I will."

He smiled, and then stood to his full height before he leaned over to softly brush his lips against hers. He whispered, "You've made me a very happy man. I'll make up for all the sadness you've had in your life."

The O'Connor account and her problems with Derek now faded into the background. Derek could take her job and the stresses that went along with it. A good strong man in her life was something she'd never had until now, and she was going to do everything in her power to be a good wife.

"I'm so happy to marry you."

"We'll all have a good life, Matthew, Gia and both of us."

∽

THREE MONTHS LATER, Jane and Zac were married. In those months preceding the wedding, Jane and Matthew had lived with an Amish family named Miller. Jane had taken the instructions to become Amish, and then she had been baptized.

Zac had reconfigured one section of the B&B to accommodate the four of them having sold the house he and Gia had once lived in with Ralene.

"How does it feel to be Mrs. Yoder?" Zac asked her on their wedding night as they stepped into their new living space.

Gia was staying with one of Zac's brothers for a couple of days, and Lizzie had put Matthew to bed a little earlier in the room beside her bedroom. Zac and Jane had arranged to get him soon, after a little time to themselves. "Wonderful, just wonderful."

Zac laughed and turned to face her. "I never dreamed when you first came here that we'd be married. You've made Gia a very happy girl and me a wondrously happy man."

"I hope so." Jane smiled as a feeling of light welled up within. "I'm a different person from the one who came here. All I cared about was being the best at what I did, and keeping the top spot." Jane giggled. "Now, I couldn't care less. You and my new family have taught me what's important."

He pulled her into his arms. "I can see it on your face that you're truly happy, and I want you to stay that way always."

She rested her head on his chest, her arms encircling him. "And I want to make you happy," she said.

He pushed her back slightly so he could look into her eyes. "I love you, Jane. You and I were meant to find each other. It's quite the love story that we can tell our children."

Jane looked into his sincere brown eyes and knew what he said was true. The tragic loss of their spouses had enabled them to meet, but she knew now it was God's hand that had brought them together. She'd thought she knew what love was before, but the love she'd had for Sean was love from the head. Her love for Zac was love from every fibre of her being.

"Tell the children we have now, or our future ones?"

He laughed. "All of them."

She flung herself back into his arms. "I hope I never lose you."

"Let's not think of things like that. We'll enjoy our days together for as long as *Gott* wills us to have them. Okay?"

"Okay." Jane held onto him tightly and sent up a silent prayer of thanks. So many things had needed to happen for them to be together, and if she'd refused to go on vacation, they never would've met. "I love you, Zac."

He held her tighter and kissed her on her forehead. "And I love you, Jane."

Thou wilt shew me the path of life:
in thy presence is fulness of joy;
at thy right hand there are pleasures for evermore.
Psalm 16:11

EXPECTANT AMISH WIDOWS

Book 1 Amish Widow's Hope
  Book 2 The Pregnant Amish Widow
  Book 3 Amish Widow's Faith
  Book 4 Their Son's Amish Baby
  Book 5 Amish Widow's Proposal
  Book 6 The Pregnant Amish Nanny
  Book 7 A Pregnant Widow's Amish Vacation
  Book 8 The Amish Firefighter's Widow
  Book 9 Amish Widow's Secret
  Book 10 The Middle-Aged Amish Widow
  Book 11 Amish Widow's Escape
  Book 12 Amish Widow's Christmas
  Book 13 Amish Widow's New Hope
  Book 14 Amish Widow's Story
  Book 15 Amish Widow's Decision
  Book 16 Amish Widow's Trust

Book 17 The Amish Potato Farmer's Widow
Book 18 Amish Widow's Tears
Book 19 Amish Widow's Heart

ABOUT SAMANTHA PRICE

USA Today Bestselling author and Kindle All Stars author, Samantha Price, wrote stories from a young age, but it wasn't until later in life she took up writing full time. Formally an artist, she exchanged her paintbrush for the computer and, many best-selling book series later, has never looked back.

Samantha is happiest on her computer lost in the world of her characters. She is best known for the *Ettie Smith Amish Mysteries* series and the *Expectant Amish Widows* series.

www.SamanthaPriceAuthor.com

Samantha loves to hear from her readers. Connect with her at:
samantha@samanthapriceauthor.com
www.facebook.com/SamanthaPriceAuthor
Follow Samantha Price on BookBub
Twitter @ AmishRomance
Instagram - SamanthaPriceAuthor